M000233235

I'm an Old Commie!

Dan Lungu

I'M AN OLD COMMIE!

Translated from the Romanian by Alistair Ian Blyth

DALKEY ARCHIVE PRESS

Originally published in Romanian by Editura Polirom
as *Sînt o babă comunistă!* in 2011.

Copyright © 2011 by Dan Lungu
Translation copyright © 2017 by Alistair Ian Blyth
First Dalkey Archive edition, 2017.

Library of Congress Cataloging-in-Publication Data
Identifiers: ISBN 9781628971484
LC Record Available at http://catalog.loc.gov/

Partially funded by a grant by the Illinois Arts Council, a state agency.

www.dalkeyarchive.com
Victoria, TX / McLean, IL / Dublin

Dalkey Archive Press publications are, in part, made possible through the
support of the University of Houston-Victoria and its programs in creative
writing, publishing, and translation.

Printed on permanent/durable acid-free paper

I'm an Old Commie!

1

FOR AN ENTIRE week . . . I've had no peace of mind for an entire week, damn it! Ever since Alice phoned . . . Alice—it's a nice name, isn't it? I chose it. Obviously, since she's my daughter. What I mean is that my husband wanted to call her something different. Christina, I think. Or maybe it was Maria. I can't remember exactly. One of those names that are ten a penny, or at least they are here, in town. The kinds of names hairdressers and bookkeepers have. No, dear, I'm going to call her Alice: a princess's name. I was dead set on it. I'd got it into my head that if you had a beautiful name, you'd have a beautiful life to match. She didn't become a princess, but an engineer. That's because I insisted on her doing a degree in engineering at university. I thought that she'd be able to get a job at the factory where I worked at the time, and that they'd all whisper to each other: Do you know that Emilia Apostoae? Well, Alice in engineering is her daughter. But before Alice could get a job there, communism collapsed and the factory where I worked went down the drain. A great big factory, but within just a couple of years it was a pile of ruins overrun with weeds and stray dogs. They stole everything, including the windows. They even ripped out the plug sockets. Now, if I happen to be passing by, I turn my head the other way. It wrenches my soul, on my word. I get the feeling that our skeletons are still inside, in our section, standing there, ready to get back to work at the drop of a hat. It's as if work has stopped only because there's a power cut. I know it's stupid, that the past is past and never returns, but that's how I feel. They say that the people

3

from Coca-Cola have bought the whole site and that they're going to open a bottling plant there. Some people are overjoyed at that. I can't imagine why. I for one don't throw my money away on poison—on rubbish like that! Every year I make elderberry lemonade the likes of which no American has ever tasted in his sweetest dreams, not even if you went back generation after generation all the way to the apes, as Mister Mitu would say. I'm going to be telling you some stories about him, too. What a wag he was! One fine day, Alice got on a plane and went to Canada. They said that the Canadians were desperate to get hold of clever people. Not that they themselves were stupid or anything, but because that great big country of theirs is inhabited by only a handful of folk. If they spread out all over the country, they'd need binoculars to see each other. They collect the brightest minds from every continent and give them a house, food, and a job. They want to make their country clever and get ahead of the Americans. I'm just saying what I've heard from other people . . . If it were up to me, I wouldn't have let her leave. I'd have kept her here with me, so that I could raise her kids and make her sweet-cheese pies on a Saturday, just the way she likes them. But I couldn't stop her. What could I tell her? Stay here, my girl, in this country that's going to hell in a handcart? Stay here and work yourself into the grave so that they can pay you a pittance? And so I didn't say anything to her. Not that she asked us. She was in such a rush to get out of here that she almost forgot she had parents. But it doesn't surprise me, because I did more or less the same thing myself when I left that hole of a village where I was born. I was even more uppity than her, if I remember rightly. Not long afterward, she phoned us to tell us she was getting married. To an Alain.

"Alain Delon?"

"Oh, come off it, Mum! Alain Delon's an old codger . . ."

"Yes, but at least folk from hereabouts have heard of him . . ."

"And besides, he's French, Mum."

"Ah, so he's from the next village," I quipped.

She informed us that she'd be coming back in the summer to

introduce him to us. "So we can have a look at the young swain, is that it?" I don't know what the custom is over there, but that's the way we do things over here. So that we can weigh him up, judge whether he's worthy of the girl.

"At least we'll be able to see whether he's missing one of his ears," says my husband, "because other than that we won't be able to understand a word of his lingo."

It must have been two or three years ago. A few days beforehand we talked over the phone about the arrangements for their arrival.

"Don't panic, he's a very nice chap," Alice said in conclusion.

Lord, how we toiled, until the house was squeaky clean! You could've eaten off the floors. I bought new curtains. I had pots boiling on every ring of the stove. The steam was rattling the lids just like in the good old days. Chicken borscht, stuffed cabbage, pork cutlets. Pies and cakes. The woman from next door helped me. For Alice's sake. And besides, she'd never seen a Canadian in her life and didn't want to miss out. Țucu, my husband, whitewashed the landing, so that the Canadian wouldn't think he'd ended up in some cave. He would have whitewashed the whole staircase, but nobody wanted to chip in any money. They could barely afford to pay their utilities bills. A neighbor from the second floor even made fun of Țucu, saying that if he'd come around scrounging money for whitewash now, the next time he'd come scrounging for a plane ticket. What an oaf! But what a loose tongue that husband of mine has! Boastful as ever, he couldn't keep his mouth shut. In his place, I'd have told the oaf that my daughter and her fiancé were swimming over, because it's cheaper, and so he shouldn't worry. The evening before, I'd been to the hairdresser's. It had been so long that I couldn't even remember when the last time was. All the hairdressers were new; none of them knew me. I don't know why, but it made me want to cry. In fact I know why. Because before the Revolution I used to go at least once a month to have my hair done. Coming home, I took a close look at the block of flats where we live. What would it look like to the guy from Canada? Wouldn't it be an embarrassment for us? The block was no longer new, like it was when we moved in, deliriously happy. More than thirty years had passed since then and it hadn't seen so much as a lick of paint in all that time. The walls were peeling, and the corners had been eaten away by the rain. On the wall above a window on the first floor, there was a thick black streak left by smoke. In the winter they'd probably put a wood stove in and stuck the flue out of the window. The steps in front of the entrance were chipped and the bannisters were bent, rattling to the touch. A thin, frowning little boy was playing outside by himself. He was tossing his woolly hat at the knobbly wall of the block of flats. When he managed to get it to stick for a few seconds, he whooped for joy. I started to panic . . . Was this the castle where Princess Alice lived? No, just one of the flats inside it.

We were exhausted. I for one could no longer feel my arms or legs. I put a pillow under my neck, so as not to mess up my hairdo. We were lying in bed and nattering before we went to sleep. Țucu was teasing me.

"You never dreamed you'd have a Canadian son-in-law . . ."

"As if you did!"

"Well, no. But I'm not proud like you . . . Who did your hair today? You ought to have bought a big curly blond wig. That would have really bowled him over!"

"It's Alice who has to bowl him over, not me!"

"Alice has already knocked him off his feet. Like a skittle. Wham! If he's prepared to come all the way to Romania . . ."

"This block of ours looks like hell!"

"We can't very well build another one by tomorrow."

"I can't get it out of my head, how bad it looks . . ."

"What'll we do if he's only got one ear?"

"One ear?"

"Our son-in-law. What if he's got only one ear?"

"You're talking nonsense. How could he have only one ear?"

"What if he's black? Did you ask what color he is? He might be black. What if he's got lips like a trumpeter's?"

"Let's go to sleep."

Țucu had got me worried with his stupid jokes. "Don't panic, he's a very nice guy," Alice had said. Why would we panic? What might make us panic? Why did she make a point of saying he was a nice guy? Did the fact that he was a nice guy make up for some defect? Țucu was making a whistling, snoring noise, and I was on tenterhooks. I couldn't sleep. In our town, a black man would be more exotic than an extraterrestrial. Even more so in our neighborhood. In our building, it would be inconceivable. And in our family . . . I preferred not to think about it. In the end, it was just a joke, I told myself, trying to take heart. Nothing was for certain. I got out of bed and went to Alice's old room. Her globe of the world was in its old place on her desk. I put my glasses on and examined it closely. No, Canada wasn't in Africa.

First thing in the morning, I went to the nearest electrical appliances shop and bought a fan. On the fourth floor where we live it's dreadfully hot. The roof stores up all the heat from the sun and releases it at night, cooking us over a low flame. I dipped into the funeral money. The "Friendship" fund, as Țucu affectionately calls it. When you get to a certain age, death becomes part of the family. You talk about it at meals or before you go to bed, you do sums. Țucu tested the fan and it worked perfectly. We had a bit of an argument about where to put it. Then we made our peace, saying that we could move it wherever it was needed. At around lunchtime, Alice phoned. They had already booked into a hotel and they invited us out for a meal. I was livid. We started squabbling.

"Why can't you understand, Mum, it's the custom over there."

"But you're over here, not over there. I even made sweetcheese pies," I said, trying to tempt her.

"There'll be time for pies too, Mum. Yum, I'm salivating already."

"Are you embarrassed to bring him to our house?"

"You're the limit! Why would I be embarrassed?"

"We've cleaned till it's spotless. Your father even whitewashed the landing . . ."

"Oh, Mum, you're so stubborn. Over there, it's perfectly ordinary to go out for a meal."

"Then do you promise you'll both come back to sleep at our house?"

"Alain has already paid for the hotel room."

"Then keep your meal! Peck it up yourselves, like two pigeons!"

"Why do you have to fly off the handle?"

"What do you mean why? You come to visit us and stay in a hotel? Do you think that's normal? Alice, we're your parents . . . Do you know what parents are? Can you still remember? We were the ones who made you and raised you."

"Yes, but . . ."

"No buts about it, please!"

"All right, I'll talk with Alain, we'll see . . ."

"Can you talk to him right now?"

We got ready to go out to the restaurant. That was the one thing we hadn't made contingencies for. I started rummaging through the cupboards, looking for clothes. Before the Revolution, when we had money by the cartload, we often used to go to parties, and so it was impossible not to find some old clothes. I'd been to umpteen engagements and baptisms. It was a kind of fashion back then. You didn't have anything to spend your money on. But godchildren were good. If you got into any bother and needed a connection at the police station or at the doctor's, you'd send the word out among your relatives and in the end you'd find the right person. In effect, my godchildren were my relatives in town, because my other relatives were all in the country. I found an ancient navy blue suit for Țucu, with white pinstripes, and a somewhat newer polka-dot frock for me. We both looked a treat, like we were tailor's dummies. That's the thing with smart clothes: if you don't wear them for a while you forget how, you don't feel comfortable in them. Or rather they used to be smart. I've never had a hat. I have pretensions to being a town-dweller, but not a lady.

2

IT'S EARLY MORNING. Everybody is busy outside. They're bustling back and forth, no time to linger. Mother calls to me whenever she passes, telling me I have to wake up. That there is a lot of work to do and the milk is going to get cold. I say, "yes, yes," and then fall asleep again every time.

In the summer all the people from our village and the neighboring villages make cow-dung briquettes. It's something I hate doing. I'm ten years old, maybe a little older. They let my younger sister sleep longer. "It's not fair!" I whisper to myself. I hear the voice of my cousin, Costicuță. You'd think he was gargling when he talked. Costicuță is a great big strapping guy, and that's why his name sounds so funny: Wee Costi. He's come to give us a helping hand. I hear the well pulley creaking. They're fetching the water already. The cocks keep crowing. It's as if they're chiding Mother. I hear heavy footfalls; I know they're not Mother's. I breathe steadily, to make it look like I'm fast asleep. It's strange that although I'm almost asleep, I'm still pretending to be asleep. In my heart of hearts I still believe that people who are fast asleep will be left to carry on sleeping. Out of pity. Like I do with sleeping cats.

My arms and legs jerk and I sit up with a start.

It's like the blast of cold water has electrocuted me.

Costicuță is already walking away, grunting with laughter.

"You're an oaf!" I shout at him furiously.

He's walking away, swinging the empty mug. Groggy, I start to get dressed. I hear laughter outside. Probably Costicuță is telling them about his exploit. The oaf! That's the only word that comes to mind this early in the morning. He's an oaf! I say it again, rolling up the sleeves of my tracksuit. The old one, not the new one. It's chilly early in the morning.

I drink my milk, my eyes still sticky with sleep. I stretch the skin of the milk on my finger, pretending it's chewing gum. The kind of chewing gum I get only from Auntie Lucreția. I catch a whiff of the cow dung, which they're turning over with their spades. The smell puts me off my food. I'm anaemic enough as it is. I don't finish my milk. I lay my hands in my lap and rest my head on my shoulder. At least let me catch a couple of minutes' sleep. Costicuță walks past, lugging two huge pails of water. Panting, he threatens to splash me again if I'm lazy. I stick my tongue out at him.

"Watch it!" he says, groaning under the weight.

Finally, I get up and in a daze I walk over to the garden at the back of the barn. Costicuță empties his two pails into a huge blue plastic barrel. Grunting, Father is shovelling up chunks of cow dung from the mound that has accumulated over the past year. The dung has settled and hardened, and so it takes him a lot of effort. They lay the chunks inside a large rectangle marked out with a stick. This is where they'll do the treading. He gives me a wink and says:

"Good morning, miss!"

In other words, I'm late.

"Don't stand there gawping! Fetch a bucket!"

"Come on, Emilia, otherwise we'll be here all day," adds Mother.

Costicuță has already come back with another pair of buckets, full to the brim. I look at him, and he sticks his tongue out at me. My mother has a bad backache, and so she can't do any carrying. With a hoe, she breaks up the clods of dung, then she picks out all the stuff that has no business being in the briquettes: sunflower and maize stalks. In disgust, I go to fetch a bucket. Father shows me where it is by casting a glance at it. It's hanging from the eaves of the barn. I've got no choice; I have to go to the well. I fetch water in a single bucket, because I'm too little to carry two. The well is in front of the house, on a small mound of earth on the other side of the fence. As I'm drawing the water, I look at the house. It's small, like something from a fairy story. If there weren't so much work to do around it, I'd find it beautiful. It has three rooms, a tile roof, and wattle and daub walls. There are pieces of brick embedded in the walls, like raisins in a cake. The bricks were from town and Father is very proud of them. He says our house is special; there aren't many like ours in the village. When I grow up, I'm going to live in a block of flats. Like Auntie Lucreţia and Uncle Andrei. Uncle Andrei is Father's older brother and he works at the train depot. He's a kind of boss. Not a big boss, but a boss all the same. Auntie Lucreţia is a telephonist and her hair is always done nicely, she always wears lipstick and perfume. She was born in the town. How lucky for her! When she sees manure, she holds her nose. Her nails are varnished. She doesn't come to visit us here in the country very often, but only occasionally, in the holidays, Mother sends me to visit her. When she does, I jump for joy. Once, I poked my nose in her basket in the bathroom and I was amazed that she doesn't just have one bottle of nail varnish, but twenty or maybe even more. Could there be a hundred? Mother says she's a bit hoity-toity and doesn't know one end of a spade from the other. That doesn't seem like a flaw to me, but I don't say anything. Mother can't stand her. Costicuţă is coming, and so I grab my bucket and quickly get moving. I carry it with both hands. It's very heavy, blasted bucket! I splash my feet, obviously. Auntie Lucreţia never goes barefoot. Not even indoors. She has slippers with pom-poms, very fluffy ones. That's why the skin of her heels isn't cracked. She loves things that are soft and fluffy. And velvety things. Halfway, at the corner of the house, I stop for a breather. I tug at a fragment of brick in the wall, which has come loose. It's almost ready to fall out. Look, it's come out of the wall. If Father catches me, he'll skin me alive. The house remains gap-toothed. But it has so many teeth nobody will notice. Our house is an animal with lots of teeth. That makes me feel like laughing. Costicuţă has filled his buckets and is heading for the yard. I grab my bucket and make tracks. I want to get there ahead of him. We're in a race, but without him knowing it. I take long strides, like an ogre. I think that maybe he's racing me without my knowing it. I go as quick as I can, but it's heavy, blasted bucket! I've soaked my legs, but we both arrive at the same time. Father is swearing. He's not happy about something. Mother has clapped her hands to her lower back. I look inside the barrel to see how much water there is. It's barely half full. Do we really need to fill it to the top?

"Come, we don't want to be here all day!" says Mother, urging us to get back to work.

I slowly make my way to the well. After I turn the corner of the barn, I put the bucket on my head, to make a German helmet. There would be room inside for four heads my size. Water trickles down the back of my neck. Brrr! Ages ago I saw a film about the Germans. At Auntie Lucreția's, obviously. We don't have electricity at our house. "I want to live in town!" I shout inside the bucket. I'm the only one who's listening. In the evening, we sit by lamplight. The glass mantle gets smoked up, especially when the flame is low and the paraffin is poor quality. It's my job to wipe the mantle, carefully, so as not to break it. When I asked Auntie Lucreția who wipes the light bulbs in her house, she laughed till she almost burst. Apparently, light bulbs never get smoked up. It's good to have light bulbs. You don't have to queue up for paraffin. "I want to live in town!" I shout down the well. I drink a mouthful of water. It's horribly cold, blasted water! We lug buckets of water until Father tells us it's enough. Then we move on to the part that I don't like at all. At all, at all. The treading. Father, Mother and me, we roll up our trousers and start to tread. Costicuță pours the water for us. We crush the manure underfoot. It's like we're dancing. We do four or five treadings every summer. Costicuță pours the water in such a way as to splash me on purpose. When only he can see, I stick my tongue out at him. Mother and Father are talking about the pig, the cow, the sheep, the fallow field, the weather, the price of milk, paraffin. We have to tread till the manure is like dough. I'm bored out of my mind. The water is very cold, blasted water! Even though it's summer, my feet feel like ice. I've pricked myself on a dratted twig. I wipe the manure off my leg to look at the scratch. Mother says that no matter how long you sift it, there'll always be splinters. Father shouts at me to keep treading, since my guts are not going to leak out of a little scratch. Sanda, my sister, has arrived. She's wearing her nightshirt. She looks at us without saying anything, like a ghost. A small, harmless ghost. A baby one. Mother sends her off to wash her face and drink her milk.

"I think it's ready," says Father. "We can add the straw."

Costicuţă unties a bale and sprinkles straw everywhere. We have to tread it in, mix it really well. I'm thinking about the mulberry tree at the bottom of the garden. I've got a secret apartment there. I pilfered a little piece of ribbon from Mother to use as a rug. If she catches me, she'll clip my lugs. I've made nail varnish bottles from the tips of corncobs. I don't have very many colors, because corncobs aren't very colorful. I've made myself hair curlers from wood shavings. I even found a triangular shard of mirror. The sink is an earthenware bowl. It's very nice there. I'm thinking that I haven't done any cleaning there for a long time. I ought to pick the fluff off the rug and wash it with vinegar. Wipe the mirror. A whole load of chores. From up in the tree, I can also see whether the Germans are invading the village. I can sound the alarm. I can alert the village policeman and get a medal. I can be a child hero. Father informs us that we can now move on to the patting. He's cleared a space by the side of the house.

"If need be, we can also lay them alongside the fence," he says.

We take lumps of manure mixed with straw, not too large, not too small, and we mold them into cake shapes. I call them scones. We lay them in the sun, lined up like soldiers. Germans or Soviets, it doesn't matter which. We place each lump on the ground and pat it with our hands. Like you would pat the cheek of someone dear to you. The sun is blazing by now. My head is scorching; my back is aching. I start moaning and griping.

"Isn't it you they'll keep warm in winter?" says Father.

Sanda has come to help with the patting. Her scones are smaller. In winter, when we put them in the stove, we can tell which ones are mine and which ones are hers. Sometimes we can guess which ones Father made. They're bigger and you can see the marks made by his fingers. Father doesn't smooth them as nicely as Mother. To me they look the same as the cowpats the cow makes across the road. I tell them this and ask why we can't just collect them like that, readymade.

"You can do that if you like, once you've got your own house," Father answers back.

"I won't need manure briquettes. I'm going to live in town," I say sulkily.

After a day like this, we sleep like lambs.

In a week, we'll have to turn them over so the other sides can dry in the sun.

3

AT THE WORKSHOP. It's been a month since I started this new job and I'm convinced that God gave me a leg up to get it. Compared with the grinding toil I've done up to now, this is a piece of cake, and the wage is twice as big. Long live Mr. Andrei! He knew a thing or two when he went out of his way to get me transferred here. I've settled in already. I know what I've got to do and I've learned the rules. On the very first day, the foreman told me:

"If you keep tight-lipped, then you'll be in clover here with me as your boss, if not, then you're out, with a kick up the backside. Nothing we do in here should go beyond these four walls . . ."

The foreman is a little guy, as thin as a plank, he talks fast and he never stands still. All day long he's like a spinning top. Coming and going, wheeling and dealing. We've got raw materials, we've got orders, we've got wages. He knows all the big shots in town and he's got dozens of connections at factories around the country. If the plant at Galaţi is crying out for sheet metal, he'll be there with a truckload. Nobody knows how he does it.

We're on our lunch break and we're sitting outside on a bench in the sun. In front of the workshop there's a vine arbor. It's not very leafy, because it's still young. Apparently it was Mister Culidiuc who planted the vines. The grapes are just about ripening. We worked hard all morning, made eight hundred brackets for the furniture factory, and so after the break we'll be taking it easy. That's what happens most days, unless an urgent order pops up. Sorin sits down on the bench. We're around the same age, except that he's been here for a year. We fall to talking and I end up praising the foreman. He nods in agreement. Then, he tells me about what happened to him with the foreman where he used to work.

Before he came here, he was at the paint factory. The atmosphere stunk really bad. Not just because of the thinners, which made you so dizzy that by the time you finished work you'd be reeling and your wife wouldn't believe you when you swore you hadn't been drinking, not just because of the thinners, like I said, but because of the personnel. The wages were low and the workers were a bad lot. They used to snitch on each other. The foreman was a nasty piece of work and he liked to know everything that went on, and so he encouraged them to stab each other in the back. Plus he was on the take.

Gaffer Pancu walks past us, with his long stiff arms hanging down, as if he were carrying two buckets of water.

If you didn't bring him presents, you could be sure not to get days off at Easter and Christmas, Sorin continues, outraged. Sorin himself didn't give him anything at all and nor did he tell any tales. One fine day, the foreman sent word for him to come to his office. With quailing heart, Sorin went. The foreman was smoking a cigarette.

"How are you, Sorin? How's life?"

"Hard at work, comrade, like everybody else."

"Look here, guy, I've got a bit of a backache, I can barely stand up, I'd like to ask you to do me a favor . . ."

"Right away, comrade."

"Nip over to the food shop and get me a hundred grams of salami, a cheese pasty, and a loaf of bread. And get me a bottle of wine, something good . . ."

Then, the foreman reached across his desk and gave him a five-bani coin.

With five bani you couldn't even buy a box of matches. Sorin gritted his teeth and bought the bastard everything he'd asked for. After he'd flung the salami and all the rest on his desk, the foreman says:

"What's this, Sorin, where's my change?"

Sorin left, slamming the door behind him.

But the story doesn't end there. Three days later, he called him back to his office to play the same trick on him. But this time it didn't work. Sorin refused to take the coin. He stopped himself from swearing at him and left. After that, the foreman sent him word that he was giving him two weeks' notice to look for another job, and even if he couldn't find another job, he'd still find some excuse to give him the sack. As there was nobody he could complain to—not that anybody would have believed him anyway—Sorin asked around and ended up here.

"Now, I'm almost grateful to the swine, because otherwise I'd never have thought of slinging my hook and leaving that place," says Sorin, smiling.

We clear up the remnants of our packed lunches and go back inside the workshop. The fun and games have started already. To pass the time, some play cards, some backgammon, some snakes and ladders. The only one doing any welding is Plugaru; he's working in a corner on what looks like a plant box. As soon as he sets eyes on Sorin, Ariton ropes him in:

"Over here, guy, the dice have been crying out for you. None of these tadpoles wants to play with me."

Sorin enters into the spirit:

"I see you're cruising for another bruising . . ."

Both of them straddle an iron bench, place the backgammon board in the middle between them, and lay out the pieces. Pancu and Costel pull up chairs, ready to give advice to the players.

"Would you look at them," says Ariton, "like crows to carrion . . . They won't risk playing, but they're champions when it comes to gawping."

"Hey, somebody switch on the machinery, so that they won't think we're in here doing nothing," shouts Radu from the other end of the workshop.

Because I'm the nearest, I get up and switch on a drill, a grinder, a perforator and the lathe. Then I go and bolt the door from the inside.

Hondrilă, a real wag whose wit has got the better of many of us, is sitting with his nose in a crossword. He's the only one here who has the patience for crosswords and he's gained a reputation for being clever. The ends of all his pencils are gnawed, in shreds even. He chews on them like bread.

"Listen up," he calls out, "whoever can guess the solution to this clue I'll give him a bottle of champagne!"

"Let's hear it then!" somebody calls back.

"It's like a riddle. Costel, are you paying attention?"

"Get on with it! Let's hear it!"

"Bronzed citizen, titchy, bandy-legged."

I think about it but nothing comes to mind. I remember that clue about the stripy napkin over the ocean, which was a rainbow.

"Well? Who gets the champagne?"

"How many letters, Hondrilă?"

"Good question. Six."

"Gypsy!"

"No, that's not it, Radu! And besides it's only got five letters."

"Then give us three-quarters of a bottle of champagne, rather than a whole one."

"All right, let me give you a hand. It's a forename . . . a first name, in other words."

"Is it from the calendar?"

"How about that! Not far off . . ."

"Bandy-legged, you say? Titchy and bronzed? Six letters? It wouldn't be our Costel, would it?" says Aurelia.

"Get out of it!" protests Costel.

"Bravo, guys! A woman's beaten you to the champagne."

True, a rabbit could easily leap through our Costel's legs: that's how bandy-legged he is. And he's a bit swarthy too. I'm miffed at not being the first to think of it. Costel is a bit upset. He gets up off his chair and goes to look at the crossword.

"Come on then, Hondrilă, show me where it says Costel. What does it say about me?"

"Costel, it's pointless getting upset. They've put you in the crossword, nothing you can do about it," laughs Radu.

"Look, here," says Hondrilă, pointing: "square by square: C-O-S-T-E-L . . ."

"Yes, but that bit about the titchy citizen with the bandy legs, where does it say that?"

"Look, here: diminutive of Constantine. That bit about the citizen I made up."

"There, you see, Hondrilă," says Costel, vindicated: "it doesn't say anything about me, does it? I may have bandy legs, but I'm not daft . . ."

At the backgammon board, the atmosphere is heating up. Ariton looks like he's foaming at the mouth, and Sorin is making a big song-and-dance. The spectators are laughing noisily. I quickly go over to watch the show.

"Look, this is how you cast the dice, Ariton, watch carefully," says Sorin, shaking the dice between his two cupped hands. He lifts his hands first to his left ear, then to his right ear. He traces a circle in the air with his joined hands, whispers something to them, like he was casting a magic spell, and then he throws the dice on the board. "Double four! What more could you wish for? That's the way to throw the dice!"

"Amazing!" exclaims Ariton. "You've eaten shit by the shovel-load ever since you were little. You really have."

"If you didn't when you were little, it's never too late," says Pancu, butting in, but Ariton ignores him, like he hasn't heard.

From what I can see, things aren't looking too good for Ariton. He needs a high throw to get past Sorin's wall otherwise he risks getting beaten soundly. He shakes the dice in his fist, without attempting any fancy stuff, and throws them. A two and a one. He clutches his head with his hands in despair.

"Didn't I just show you how it's done? For God's sake!" Sorin teases him.

"I say you should give it up, Ariton. Go to the National Commission of Backgammon Players and lay your resignation on the table, signed and stamped."

"What an attentive guy you are, Pancu! You always bring me bad luck whenever you're around."

"Do you know why? Because I've got a black cat here in my pocket, and in my mind I keep repeating: thirteen, thirteen, thirteen . . ."

"You're full of it when you're just sitting and watching, but when yours truly gave you a real drubbing, you had a face as long as a horse's . . ."

"That was then, this is now."

"With throws of the dice like he got, you'd have to be stupid not to win!" says Ariton, consoling himself.

"What do you say to another round?" asks Sorin, stretching his shoulders to limber up.

"I'll give Pancu a turn. You'll make mincemeat of him."

"What do you say, Pancu?"

"I say you're playing with fire, laddie!" says Pancu, getting up off his chair and straddling the metal bench.

4

ALICE WAVED TO us from a distance. She ran up to us. Tears almost came to my eyes. When I hugged her, I could feel she'd fleshed out. She must be living well. Ultimately, that's the most important thing. Alain didn't kiss my hand. I'm not saying he should have kissed his prospective father-in-law's hand, because people don't do that anymore, not even here. We're the last generation to have kissed our parents' hands. What can I say: it was a burden off my heart when I saw my son-in-law wasn't black. The globe was right: Canada isn't in Africa. He also had two ears, thank the Lord! It was wonderful that he did. He was a little pale, with whitish eyelashes and eyebrows. A tad taller than Alice. He had thinning hair, which means he'll go bald quickly. He said *bună ziua* to us, which I liked. He looked a bit fragile. Delicate. Țucu almost ripped his arm from his socket when he shook his hand. Mind you don't break him, I said to myself, chiding him in my mind. Not knowing how to speak the language, the poor guy kept smiling all the time. He had nice teeth, white and straight. It was obvious his parents had taken care of his teeth, that they'd stuffed him with calcium and made him brush twice a day. He probably comes from a good family, I said to myself. He wasn't well-built, but nor was he weedy. His liver seemed to be in working order, and he sipped his wine rather than knocking it back. I admit I kept looking him up and down, like a horse trader at the fair. It was as if an instinct awakened in me, like an animal that wants its cub to be safe. I think it's an instinct mothers have, because the next day if you'd asked Țucu to describe his son-in-law, he'd

23

have said he had two ears. I wanted my Alice to have a nice
family. If she'd started out with a sickly man with bad habits,
she'd have had a life of suffering in store. All in all, Alain made
a good impression. He was very tender toward her. He looked
at her lovingly and pandered to her every whim. He treated her
like a princess. It wasn't for nothing that I called her that: Alice.
But apart from tenderness, in my opinion health is important
too. Not even tenderness can rescue a man who's in and out of
hospital all the time. I can't conceive of a man who's unable to
give his child a piggyback. I'd give him bad marks for the way
he was dressed. You'd have thought our Alain was going to the
disco. He was wearing a pair of jeans and a short-sleeved shirt.
On his feet he had trainers. I don't know how they go about
things over there, but over here you don't dress like that when
you're coming to ask for a girl's hand. Were those the best
clothes he had? Țucu was sweating like an ox in his pinstriped
suit, and my eyes were popping because of a seam that kept
digging into my flesh. An old biddy suffering so that she could
look nice! Alice was as fresh as a flower and was all smiles. She
was a bit jowly. It's obvious that she's living well. She was
dressed nicely, with a light linen frock, and on her feet she had
a nice pair of sandals. Not that I'm boasting or anything, but
she's inherited her good taste from me. You could dress Țucu
in a sack and send him into town; it wouldn't make any difference to him.

I don't even want to remember the food. Alain ordered a salad
and two scrawny fish with a slice of lemon. I was worried he
might be on a diet. I thought I must have been mistaken about
his liver. But apparently that's the way he eats: frugally, dieteti-
cally. That's why people over there live till they're ninety. Their
children reach retirement before they come into their inheri-
tance. When they retire they're well off and they start traveling
around the world. Them and the Japanese. Țucu ordered tripe
soup and grilled pork with fried potatoes. I didn't feel much like
eating and so I ordered five skinless sausages and mustard. Alice,
the poor thing, didn't get a chance to eat, because she kept having to translate, now for us, now for him. She ordered fish too.

So she'd be the same as him, no doubt. It was then that I saw for the first time that with a foreigner you don't have much to talk about. He minds his own business; we mind ours. He's not interested in our beggarly pensions, and we've got no idea how things are over there. What can I say? It was quite awkward. Alain said that there are still a lot of things that need fixing in Romania, but that it's a beautiful country. We knew that already. He asked what it was like under communism. When I told him that I was worse off now than I was before the Revolution, he stared in amazement and asked: "Why?" My husband nudged me under the table. How could I explain it to him? I'd have had to talk all through the night till the next morning to make him understand. I'd have had to tell him my whole life story. Then he said that he was happy that Ceaușescu was deposed, because he wouldn't have met Alice otherwise. And he laughed. He was right on that score.

In the evening we all went to our house. Even though the windows were wide open, it was as hot as in a bakery. I switched the new fan on and congratulated myself on the idea. Țucu was the only one who ate the broth and steak I'd made. Alice wolfed down two sweet-cheese pies, and Alain pecked up the crumbs she left. He didn't even want to try the plum brandy. At his request, I made him some iced mint tea. I can't say it was nice, but it was a family occasion. They went to bed early, and we stayed up watching TV.

"Listen, do you know what I was thinking?"
    "Hmm?"
    "That guy, Alin . . ."
    "Alain!"
    "I call him Alin. Leave me be!"
    "What about him?"
    "Well, that guy, if you made him push a wheelbarrow of bricks, he'd pass out after ten meters."
    "So?"
    "I was just saying . . ."

"Why would he have to lug bricks if he works in a bank?"
"Hmm, maybe you're right."
Then we both fell asleep.

The next day, the kids went off to visit the monasteries of northern Bukovina. Alain was sick all the way. Because of the difference in the water, that's what I say.

Then they went back to Canada. If I think about it, Alain still hasn't asked for the girl's hand. It's as if they just came on holiday. Or maybe they have different customs over there. But then Alice is guilty. She should have explained to him that over there it's one thing and over here quite another. Then they had the wedding. They wanted to pay for our plane tickets so that we could come, but I get travel sickness riding a bicycle, let alone flying. Thickheaded as he is, Țucu would have gone. Go on then, go flying through the air, I said to him. Maybe you want to see how cozy it is in the belly of a shark. In any case, he couldn't have gone because he had to look after the animals. Oh, the countless arguments we've had about that! After the Revolution, his factory went down the drain, like so many others. And so he found himself on his uppers. He tried to find another job, but no such luck. He was too old to go to Italy and work laying floor tiles. Since his parents had died before '89, one of his sisters, Catrina, looked after the family smallholding. And so what did our Țucu decide to do? He decided to go back to the country and raise poultry and piglets . . . Especially since it's close to the town, twenty kilometers away, and there are buses every hour. I mean! I reacted like a scalded cat. I made it quite clear to him:
"I know I'm not rolling in money living here in town, but I'm not going back to the country."
It was a difficult moment. We quarreled with each other for about two months. We had hardly any money, life was getting more and more expensive, and so we made a deal: he would go to the country a few days a week, and I would stay here, in the apartment. Things evened out somehow, although every time he comes back the smell of manure has seeped into his clothes. I

can smell it. If I'd gone back to the country, it would have been as if I'd lived in vain. I would have been going back to where I started. It would have been as if I'd run away from home for nothing, as if I'd gone back, long years later, with my tail between my legs. The very thought of it roused in me all the anger I'd felt as a child, it awakened the fear of being labeled the village idiot. Now, after so many years of marriage, I can admit that I wasn't an easy catch. Poor Ţucu courted me for months and months and I barely looked twice at him. I liked him, because he was smartly dressed back then, he was well kempt and smelled of aftershave, he had a sense of humor and used to talk about the films that were on at the cinema, but he had a single fault: he was from the country. I wanted a man from town, one who'd never walked barefoot in his life. Even though he behaved exactly like the young people from town—because a village twenty kilometers away is completely different from one seventy kilometers away—I knew for sure that he was from the country; the girls I shared a room with had told me. I lived in a hostel for spinsters at the time. He tried all kinds of things to win me and couldn't understand why I was as cold as ice. When he visited our room at the hostel, it was always a festive occasion. He would bring fruit juice, ice cream and cakes for everybody. In other words he pretended he wasn't coming because of me, but just to visit the girls. He'd known one of them for a long time; they'd been at school together. But obviously all the girls knew that I was the target. He used to tell such funny stories that they'd end up rolling around the floor with laughter. But I would barely smile, although after he left I sometimes burst out laughing when I remembered his jokes. The thing that puzzled him the most was that I wasn't going out with anybody else, because then it would have been understandable. He'd asked the girls if I had a boyfriend, they told him I hadn't, but they also reported to me everything he asked. I carried on a kind of correspondence through them. If I wanted to tell him something, it was enough for me to reveal it to one of my room-mates, as if by accident, when we were nattering among our-selves. Once, without intending anything by it, I said that I loved apricots. The next day, besides juice and cakes, Țucu turned up with a bag of apricots. The telegraph wire worked perfectly. I think that the girls were also curious to see how long I would hold out and above all why. I never told them the real reason. I always told them that I just wasn't ready to get married, although at that age it was about time. "Maybe you're waiting for a prince on a white horse," they used to say, laughing at me. I remember that it was getting close to my birthday. I wasn't excited about it or anything, because nothing much used to happen: I used to go out for a quiet drink with my roommates. I didn't receive many cards, because I never used to go around telling everybody it was my birthday. Well, that year, as soon as I left my room at the hostel, everybody I met wished me a happy birthday, with obvious amusement. I was surprised, but I told myself that the girls must have been telling people. Even the concierge wished me a happy birthday. That rascal Țucu had talked to some painter friend of his and had plastered posters all over the hostel. It was a picture of my face and above it said "Wanted," like in the cowboy films when the sheriff is looking for a bad guy, and underneath it said: "If you see this person today, wish her a Happy Birthday." Back then there weren't any photocopiers, not like today; all the posters were handmade. The picture of me was quite a good likeness. I think it must have been copied from a photograph. To this day I haven't discovered which of the girls was the traitor who supplied the photograph. I was annoyed, but also amused. The next week, I agreed to go out with him, just so that I could find out whom he'd plotted it with. But Țucu kept the secret. On the other hand, I found out that in his village they don't make manure briquettes, and so without my noticing it I started to find him more likeable. We continued to go out every now and then, without my making any plans for the future. All the time I was on the look out for his flaws, or in other words, the habits of a boy from the country. I even studied the way he sneezed. I had noticed that folk born and bred in town didn't make a noise when they sneezed, so that it echoed over hill and vale, as if a loud sneeze were a sign of good health, but rather they covered their mouths with their hands and half swallowed the sneeze. Well, Țucu sneezed like a town-dweller. In the end I had to accept that it wasn't his fault if he'd been born in the country. And anyway, it was only twenty kilometers from town. And so we got married. It is only now, with the arrival of old age and all its misfortunes, that my Țucu has discovered his peasant leanings, but by now it's too late. In any event, that's what I told him, when he wanted us both to move lock, stock and barrel: he won't catch me in the country, except as a visitor.

Alice and Alain sent us photographs of the wedding. You wouldn't even think they were taken in Canada: chairs like over here, tables like over here, people with two arms and two legs. The only way you can tell it wasn't a one-hundred-percent Romanian wedding is from the puny fish on the plates. If some real stuffed cabbage had been plonked in front of them, then I reckon they would have been fighting each other for seconds. But what I liked the most was that over there, the bride wears a bridal gown, and Alice looked like a lily in full bloom. A week ago Catrina came to see us and we showed her the photographs. She looked at them without saying anything, and after that she began to cry. "What's up with you?" I asked her. She waved her hand to show that it was nothing. She talked about other things for a quarter of an hour and it was only then that she confessed that she cried when she saw how beautiful Alice looked dressed in white. She has a son, but she really wanted a girl. In her heart, she adopted Alice. She saved up money for her wedding and she still has it. She desperately wanted to see her as a bride. When I told her that Alice is expecting a baby, she cried her eyes out.

Then she talked about my and Țucu's wedding, digging up all kinds of memories for me too.

By the time I got married, I'd made my peace with my parents, but they still hoped that I would return to the village. In fact, I think that was one of the reasons why we made our peace. If they'd kept on being angry with me, there would never have been any hope of my coming back, but if they reached out to me, there was still a chance. I think that Uncle Andrei advised them to do that, but I'm sure that it was Auntie Lucreția who was behind it. We made our peace, but they didn't forgive me. That suited me very well. When they heard that I wanted to get married in the town, they knew they wouldn't be able to bring me back. And so they weren't very enthusiastic about the impending wedding. Before I took Țucu with me to introduce him, I tried to coach him, but he didn't listen to me and he got along much better than if I'd been able to teach him. We stayed with them three days. On the first day, he showed them how neat and polite he was, without putting on any hoity-toity town airs. The second day, he went to visit the farm with Mother and Father, he praised their piglets and hens, he petted the cow, and he showed a keen interest in techniques for manufacturing manure briquettes, the rascal. And the third day, he asked them for some old clothes and despite their half-hearted protests, he lent a hand with the farm chores. By the time we left, their only regret was that Țucu wasn't a guy from their village. I even think they'd have preferred to have him for a son than me for their daughter. Even so, they weren't very merry at the wedding. But at least they came.

Catrina was fuming at Țucu. Apparently, since he started coming, their parents' farm had been a shambles. He didn't sow on time, he didn't water the crops, he didn't hoe, and he didn't harvest on time. He made out that he knew it all, but he always got things mixed up. Half the hens had died, and you had to go begging to the ones that survived before they'd lay an egg. In the summer he hadn't pruned the tomatoes. And so they were like great big bushes and the tomatoes were as big as cherries. The carrots were tiny too. The weeds had sprouted as high as maize. The plum trees were full of caterpillars. The apples were as big as walnuts.

"You pretend you're a peasant, but the whole village is laughing at you!" said she.

In other words, I'd been right to choose him all those years ago.

5

I'm in town! I'm in town, hooray! At Auntie Lucreția's and
Uncle Andrei's. They go off to work in the morning and I have
the whole house to myself. In the morning, the house is all
mine. They don't leave me much to do. I have to air the rooms
and make the beds. I have to wash the dishes, and sweep the
floors if need be. I have to dust the furniture. And the bibelots.
They have lots of bibelots. Most of all I like the stork that looks
like he's about to take wing. You'd think he's about to break
loose and hit his head on the ceiling. He falls over and I patch
him up. I do a good deed. When I'm in a fix he'll help me too.
If I'm ever on a desert island with no hope of rescue, my stork
will fly to me and take me to the nearest town. I pick the bits
of fluff off the rug and wash it with vinegar. I gather in the
washing hung out to dry on the balcony. I wash the sink in the
bathroom. I wipe the mirror. I scrub the tiles. What a difference
there is between their bathroom and our outside toilet! The
wind blows between the planks of the outside toilet. In winter,
the snow gets inside. I wash all the shoes and then polish them.
What a lot of shoes Uncle Andrei has got! What a lot of sandals
Auntie Lucreția has got! They must have paid heaps of money
for them. In town the people have lots of money. Where we live,
in the country, there is so little money that Mother can tie it up
in a handkerchief. Mother wears rubber boots and Father wears
bast shoes. Money doesn't go far, Mother always says. It goes on
paraffin, salt, sugar, cooking oil, and school exercise books. Does
money go any further in town? Sometimes we even buy bread.
When Mother doesn't feel well enough to bake any. In town,

people have enough money to buy dessert. Sweets, I mean. Sometimes they even buy fruit. In the country the fruit grows on trees, we don't spend money on it. At least we've got that much! Ah, I need to feed Fluff. Auntie Lucreția left some soup and a little bit of meat for her. Fluff is fluffy. That's how she got her name. She isn't a mongrel; she's a noble breed. I think she comes from a family of princes and her ancestors lived in a castle. That's why she's very clean and very fussy. Like Auntie Lucreția. They could be sisters. In our village the people don't look after themselves. When they leave the house, they don't leave a scent of perfume in their wake. I think perfume must cost money. They always have dirty feet and the backs of their shirts are always wet, like they've been lugging a block of ice. The cleanest person in our village is Comrade Teacher Sebastian Protopopescu. He wears a suit and a tie and his shoes are shiny. But he wasn't born in our village; he's an incomer. We do mathematics with him. He's very clever. He can do sums in his head. Not even the comrade director is as clean as he is; there are always bits of straw on his clothes. Once he even forgot to zip up his trousers. When we come home from school, we children have to do chores on the farm. We water the animals and unload hay. Comrade Teacher Sebastian Protopopescu doesn't do anything like that. At most, we see him smoking. They say he's so clever that ages ago he taught at a university. Before he came to our village, obviously. I was surprised that he came to our school and so I asked my father about it. Father didn't really know, but he said he must be an enemy of the people. He didn't support the communists, in other words. Maybe he was part of the king's camarilla or a member of the Iron Guard. Or maybe something else happened. He didn't look like much of an enemy to me. He used to speak to us nicely and he was always well shaven.

"So why did they send him to our village?"

"As a punishment."

"Do people have to live in our village as a punishment? Is it like a prison?"

"I don't know. Ask your ma!"

I don't want to be punished. I want to live in town. I'm not an enemy of the people. But all the same, how can an enemy of the people be so clever? And what does "enemy of the people" mean anyway? I imagined that Comrade Teacher Sebastian Protopopescu was on one side and the people were on the other. The one side was an enemy of the other. He didn't love them. The people are like a man with lots of heads, arms and legs. If it came to a fight, Comrade Teacher Sebastian Protopopescu wouldn't stand a chance, no matter how clever he might be. But the comrade teacher doesn't have the face of an enemy. Maybe a change comes over him at night. Maybe he grows horns and sharp claws. Maybe even tusks like an elephant's. Then he'd be able to fight the people. But only at night. In the bathroom, I come across the bottles of nail varnish again. In the little basket. The bottles are like castles for pixies. Once, Auntie Lucreția did my nails for me. She was laughing and asked me whether I liked it. After that I couldn't stop looking at my nails, even when we were eating. She said that she was going to make a townie out of me, because I was cut out for it. But she didn't keep her word. About a week later, she took me back to the country. But when I was with her in town, she bought me a hat, which I lost in the grain wagon afterward. I like to go into town with Auntie Lucreția. She buys me ice cream and juice. And chocolate. She spends a whole load of money. Think of how much paraffin and salt you could buy for that money! We don't use much salt, but the sheep do. All winter long they lick boulders of salt. You'd think they were sharpening their tongues. They like it. And so do the goats, I think. That's why the nanny goat brings her three kids a block of salt in the fairy tale, lugging it on her back. The towels in the bathroom are soft. I like to press my face against them. It's nice to do the cleaning in town. You can think of all kinds of things while you're doing it. It's not hard at all. You don't have to fetch water in a bucket; it comes out of the tap. You can fill a cup, a bucket or a barrel, as much as you like. You can fill the tub and take a bath. We get washed in a wooden trough. In summer we leave it full of water so that the sun will warm it up. It's harder in winter. It's a big chore to heat the water on the stove. Even though people are cleaner in town, they take baths more often. That I don't understand. In the bathtub you can lie back or even swim. In the trough you have to crouch or kneel. No question of splashing around in it. Once Auntie Lucreţia took me with her to where she works. It was wonderful. She and another two or three women sit there wearing headphones and plug wires into lots of different sockets. Auntie Lucreţia knew where every wire had to go. She swapped them around. "Depending on the connection," she explained. She talked continuously. "Bălţaţi? Bălţaţi, can you hear me? You have now been put through. Long live the Struggle for Peace!" "Hello, Costeşti? Can you hear me? You are through to Hîrtoapele. Long live the Romanian People's Republic" or "Long live the Romanian proletariat!" That's all she said. But everything was very clean and her nails were as red as could be. Sometimes she talked in her sleep, giving me a fright. In a metallic voice, like at work. I heard her from the next room. She was making connections and wishing the people at the other end of the line something to do with brotherhood between nations. She knew lots of people, Auntie Lucreţia did. After we left the place where she worked, she took me to the Three Bears cake shop. Another time I went into town with Uncle Andrei. To the train station. Not to the ticket office, but to a place they called the ramp. Everybody said hello to him. Especially the workers loading the freight cars. Uncle Andrei had a notebook and he was always writing things down. A man turned up, who spoke a foreign language. Russian. I've always wondered why the Soviets speak Russian and not Soviet. The man was called Volodya. Comrade Volodya. Comrade Volodya called Andrei Vasya. Uncle Andrei was speaking now Romanian, now Russian. I never knew that Uncle Andrei had two names. Andrei and Vasya, that is. The workers were loading grain. Lord, the amount of grain that was there!

"What can you do with so much grain?" I asked him.

Uncle Andrei laughed and tousled my hair. He explained it to me patiently, looking at Comrade Volodya, who was smiling. I understood that in our country the wheat we have isn't very good. The grains are too small and they spoil quickly. But in the

Soviet Union the scientists have invented a much better kind of wheat. That's why the Soviets, like older brothers, decided to help us. We give them five wagons of bad grain, and they give us one wagon of good grain, for seed. But in fact the good grain is worth much more, because you can't find it anywhere else in the world. In a few years we'll have wheat just as good as theirs. That's what happens when older brothers help their younger brothers. Comrade Volodya nodded his head: yes, that's right. After Comrade Volodya left, Uncle Andrei allowed me to climb into a grain wagon to play. I waded into the grain up to my knickers. Then I swam. Afterward I was very sorry that I went in there, because I lost my hat inside. I cried all night because of that. I told Uncle Andrei that I remembered exactly where I'd left it. I'd hung it from a screw in the wagon. Because I was afraid I might get it dirty. But Uncle Andrei told me there was nothing he could do about it. Because the wagons have been sealed, ready to leave. Maybe they've left already . . . I just have to clean the cooker and then I'm done! If I sit here pressing my face to this soft towel any longer, I might fall asleep.

6

TWO LONG KNOCKS followed by one short inform us that somebody we know is at the door. We don't bother ourselves, but
merely wonder who it might be. Somebody draws the bolt and
the foreman comes in with a crate of beer.

"That's enough, kids, come on, we've got work to do! There's
a van outside with fifty beds to unload."

Nobody says anything. We put away our games and get
organized. Apparently the beds are from a boarding lyceum
and we have to get them ready for the start of the new school
year. We have to repair and paint them. And as quickly as possible. We have to work overtime to finish them, because they
have to dry overnight and be taken back tomorrow. The
unloading doesn't take long. They're metal beds with folding
legs, and so they're easy to handle. One of the gatekeepers, the
youngest, lends us a hand. At our factory there are three gates:
the main gate and two side gates. Our workshop is right next
to one of the side gates, the one by which the heavy vehicles
usually enter. So as not to go all the way around, we enter by
that gate in the morning, which is why the gatekeepers know
us well.

The foreman examines the beds on every side. He tells us
what we have to do. There's not much that needs repairing: some
loose rivets here and there, some cracked welds, a spring or two
missing.

"They're well behaved, them boarders," says the foreman,
with a smile. "They haven't put a strain on the beds . . ."

"Oho, when I was at lyceum . . ." says Ariton.

"When were you at lyceum, eh? I thought you had just two years' schooling more than a train," quips Pancu.

"I was at two lyceums, not just one, if you really want to know. The one on Viilor Street and the one on Naţională . . ."

"Look at the genius hiding in our midst!"

"Brick by brick I built them . . . I worked in construction at the time."

We sort the good beds from the ones that need repairing and then we form two teams. Deciding on the two teams is hard, because nobody wants to do the painting. It's tricky and uncomfortable. And then there's the smell of the thinners, which make your head spin. The girls, Aurelia and me, that is, are assigned to the brushwork from the start, because we're supposed to have the most patience. Hondrilă volunteers. Sorin won't even hear of it; he's sick to the back teeth of paint. Finally, Radu gives in, on the condition that he gets extra beer at the end. After making sure we're organized, the foreman vanishes with the man from the boarding lyceum, probably the administrator.

Hondrilă takes us aside and explains his plan. Aurelia and Radu are keen on it, but I'm a bit wary:

"We'd need a huge amount of paint for that."

"Is that your problem? Haven't we got paint?" laughs Hondrilă.

No sooner said than done. We cobble together a sheet metal tank, a little larger than the size of a bed and some forty centimeters deep. That was a piece of cake. We fetch a vat of paint and fill the tank three quarters. Then, we start baptizing the beds. Two people are all that's needed. With two grappling hooks, each lifts one end of the bed, with its legs folded, and dips it in the tank of paint. We hang the hooks from the rail of the mobile crane in the yard: the small crane we use for unloading bales of sheet metal from the trucks. Hondrilă and Aurelia do five beds, then Radu and me do five, and so on. We spread newspapers underneath to catch the paint drips. We've got newspapers aplenty, because we're all subscribers to *The Spark*, the Party newspaper. It's compulsory; they deduct the subscription from our wages. We barely glance at the papers. Most of them have never even been opened. I take copies to the country, where they use them to light the fire. The paint is pouring off the beds, but the work is going briskly. The people repairing them can't keep up with us, at the rate we're baptizing them.

"Long, frequent breaks, that's the key to success," says Aurelia.

Hondrilă continues his crossword, and Radu nips back inside to take the mickey out of the guys who didn't want to do the painting. I remind Aurelia that she promised me a kilo of oranges. Her husband works in the stores at a good shop, and so he gets to handle all kinds of goodies. She tells me what happened to her husband. They'd received a large consignment of goods, including even oranges. So that the windows of the shop wouldn't get broken in the crush, they were selling the oranges at the back door. A line like you wouldn't believe. A huge crowd. Lots of old folk with their grandchildren. It was obvious that there wasn't enough to go round, and so they told the people at the back to go home, because there was no point in their standing in line. But nobody budged. The people at the back told them to stop giving the people at the front a whole kilo, but just half a kilo instead. But it's harder to weigh out half-kilos, and the people at the front started kicking up a fuss, because they'd been waiting for ages and they wanted it at least to have been worth their while. The situation was getting quite tense. Obviously, the people who work at the shop had set three crates aside, to share among themselves after closing time. While they were trying to appease the people at the back, a bigwig from the Securitate, who happened to be passing, talked to the head of the shop and told him to give him a crate of oranges. As if he couldn't have got one from the Party canteen or elsewhere. But no, he wanted a crate from the shop and he wanted it right then and there. The boss of the shop didn't have any choice and so he gave him one. The arrogant bigwig didn't want to pull up in front of the shop and slip the crate in the trunk of his car. Instead, he got his chauffeur to lug the crate to the car park. Obviously, everybody saw him and started shouting. But the bigwig had slung his hook, and the people from the shop had to deal

with the aftermath. Five guys from the line formed a kind of delegation and forced their way into the shop to check what goods
were inside. There was pushing and shoving. There were threats
on both sides. The citizens were so angry that they were on the
verge of beating up the people in the storeroom. In the end, they
found the two crates that had been put aside, not that it altered
the situation, as there still weren't enough oranges to go around.
The people in the line argued among themselves and in the end
they demanded that each person be sold one orange, and that
those with children should be given priority. And so poor Aurelia's
husband had to spend hours selling individual oranges, under the
belligerent eyes of the customers. He got the nastiest looks from
the children, who had been told that the man from the shop stole
their oranges and that was why there weren't enough for them.

And that's why she hadn't brought me the oranges she
promised.

I nod in sympathy and she says that maybe next week . . .

"What about bananas?" I ask.

"Oho, they're like hens' teeth."

Later on, the foreman turns up in an Aro jeep with the administrator. They back it up to the door of the workshop and signal
two guys to unload it. Then the foreman and the administrator
make an inspection. The man from the lyceum nods in satisfac-
tion and says:

"There's no need to paint the part on which the mattress
rests."

"It's nicer like that, because they won't rust," says the foreman, giving us a wink.

After the two talk among themselves, making the arrangements for tomorrow, the man who I think must be the administrator climbs into the Aro and leaves. The foreman calls us all
inside. On the workbench, which is spread with plastic sheeting,
Culidiuc has started cutting up the second pig.

"Them pigs are fed on leftovers from the canteen. Look at the
meat on them!" he says.

He knows what he's talking about. He's got a sty in his back yard. We take a headcount and start sharing out the meat. The best cuts are set to one side for the foreman. Culidiuc wipes up the blood with a rag and wrings it out over a bucket. He asks for a beer.

"Hey, don't forget the gatekeepers. Give them a share too."

We divvy up once more. There's enough for everybody. I watch in amazement. To the others it's nothing unusual. They remember the cheeses, the barrels of cooking oil and the sacks of Carpați cigarettes they've shared out on other occasions.

I go home, happy, carrying ten kilos of meat.

When he sees what's in the bag, Țucu whistles:

"Whoa, did you burgle a butcher's shop?"

7

AFTER CATRINA LEFT, I couldn't stop thinking about the past. I puttered around the house muttering to myself. When you're getting on in years, it's nice to do that. You clean the slate with different people, you come up with the replies that you couldn't think of at the time, you smile at the nice memories, you go over the sequence of events however many times you like, to grasp why things turned out the way they did and not otherwise. Your whole life is there with you in the same room. Your plans have to do with the past rather than the future. You keep rearranging the same pieces of the puzzle, without getting bored of it for a single minute. It's the same with children, and Alice was no exception: they like to listen to the same story over and over again. You're only interested in talking to people of the same age, because that's the only way you can find new pieces to fit the puzzle, which are getting scarcer and scarcer. And if the past was wonderful, whereas the present is a disaster, then talking to yourself becomes a necessity.

When the phone rang, I was in the middle of giving Țucu a tongue-lashing for leaving a pair of socks on the floor, despite the fact that he wasn't there to hear it. At that hour of the day it could only be Alice. Ever since she got pregnant she'd been phoning more often than before. I was right: it was her. She sounded lively, a sign that things were going well for her.

"How are you, Mum? Haven't you gone to bed?"

"I was just nagging your father . . ."

"Really? Put him on the phone."

"Why, do you want to nag him a bit, too?"

"Well, not really. I trust you. I just wanted to see how he's doing."

"Your father's outside with his hens. I was nagging him for leaving his socks all over the place."

"Ah, I get it . . . Make sure you stay angry until he gets back . . ."

"Better you tell me how that little Canadian of yours is doing."

"He keeps moving around in my tummy . . . Yesterday I felt a heel."

"I hope you're eating well."

"I'm eating, I'm eating . . . but it's exhausting. He's mad about calcium, especially the calcium in my teeth. It probably tastes better."

"Are you having trouble with your teeth?"

"I've cracked a molar."

"Be more careful!"

"Say, Mum, who will you be voting for on Sunday? That's also why I'm phoning."

"Is that what's keeping you awake at night in Canada? Not knowing who I'll be voting for?"

"It isn't a major international issue yet. Ha, ha! I just wanted to know . . . Go on, tell me!"

"Will you be voting?"

"Of course, at the embassy . . . Tell me!"

"Oho, Sunday is still a long way off . . . I've got plenty of time to decide and to change my mind a hundred times . . ."

"Humph, you're stringing me along. Let me explain it to you. I'm a member of a Romanian association here, and we've all decided to do our bit for the elections in Romania . . . and so each of us has to talk to two or three people, however many we know, and persuade them to vote for democracy."

"In other words, you're canvassing?"

"Well, not really . . . The idea isn't to persuade people to vote for a certain party, but to persuade them not to vote for the ex-communists."

"Is that so? Then who should they vote for, Pope Pius?"

"Come on, Mum, I'm being serious."

"What, and I'm joking, am I? As far as I'm concerned, things are very simple: before the Revolution, I had a much, much better life than I do now. Whom would you vote for in my shoes?"

"I think you're exaggerating when you say 'much, much better,' Mum. Have you forgotten the meat lines? They stretched all the way around the block . . ."

"True, there were lines back then, but nowadays you go to the shops, you admire the cutlets, you drool, and then you go away again, because you don't have any money to buy them. Or else you can stand and watch while some nouveau riche buys two kilos of steak. I don't know when was better . . . On the television I see people dying of hunger, families with children sleeping on the street . . . That kind of thing never happened in the days of communism."

"It will sort itself out in the end . . . We're still in the transition period . . . but I'm optimistic."

"It's easy to be optimistic when you live in Canada, in France, or in America . . . It's harder to be optimistic when you're here and you have to live through it. Then you'll find out the meaning of the word optimism!"

"Come on, Mum, I know very well what the situation is like . . ."

"Do you now! And I know the situation of the foreman who steals the whole factory when it gets privatized, but we don't put the same meal on the dinner table."

"What about freedom, Mum? You can't compare that with anything else. Back then we were afraid of even our own shadows. The fact that now you can say what you want and write what you want, you can travel, you can shout 'Down with the Government!' . . ."

"You know what, it's the people who got rich overnight who travel, the people who stole everything we worked for. As for shouting, you can shout as much as you like, because nobody's listening anyway . . . If it were up to me, I'd bring back communism tomorrow."

"Really, Mum! I thought you were pretending, but you're more of a communist than I thought!"

"Well, I've shown my true colors, haven't I then? I'm an old commie, if you really want to know. That's what I am."

"What if Ceaușescu were standing as a candidate on Sunday, would you vote for him?"

"I haven't thought about it. But if my former foreman were standing, I'd elect him president. He knew how to bring in the orders . . . He knew how to treat people decently . . . He looked after us each and every one . . . The way he ran our shift, he would be able to run a country."

"All right, I get the point. But what did communism ever do for you, Mum? Why is it you can't let it go? Apart from lies, terror, lines, cold . . . what else did it ever do?"

"I'm talking about my life, Alice, not other people's. Above all else, communism made me a townie."

"Unless . . ."

"Let me finish. If they hadn't built factories, roads, flats, but above all factories, then the two of us, Emilia and Alice, would be trampling dung for fuel, until the eyes popped out of our heads, somewhere in some village down a dirt track."

"I don't agree. If the capitalists had been in power, they'd have been able to do even more . . ."

"In the end it was the communists who did it. If the capitalists had done it, I'd have been on their side . . . As well as a job, the communists gave me a flat and a gas canister . . . Free of charge, mind you."

"A matchbox, Mum, not a flat."

"Whatever you say, girl. But it was big enough to raise a child in, a child who became clever and pretty enough to get married in Canada."

"Tugging at the heartstrings, eh?"

"Old commie that I am, I'm good at propaganda. I almost got into the Party School."

"Look, Mum, just like you're talking from your own experience, there's something I can tell you from my own experience: I don't have a single reason to pine for communism. If the

Revolution hadn't come, I'd have been a lowly engineer in some grimy factory in some godforsaken town; I'd have lived in a matchbox with a view of a patch of waste ground or a graveyard . . . Oh, yes, I almost forgot: I'd have had a gas canister. Look what I missed out on!"

"Yes, well, I think you'd have got along just fine at one of the Party Schools. But, mind you, a lot of young people today, right here in our building, pine for communism . . ."

"I told you, I'm speaking for myself. And maybe for the other young people who left the country . . ."

"Maybe some of them ought to be thankful to Ceaușescu . . . If he hadn't outlawed abortions, they wouldn't have been born to be able to curse him now . . ."

"It's horrid what you're saying, Mum!"

"But that's how things were, wasn't it! Not in your case, though, you were wanted . . ."

"And if Ceaușescu had ruled another ten years, all those children you're talking about would have had bellies swollen with hunger . . ."

"You'll be running up a really huge phone bill there . . ."

"Don't worry about it. The phone bills are cheap here in the decadent West . . . Tell me what you're going to do about voting."

"Well, what can I do . . ."

"What shall I tell the people from the association?"

"Just tell them straight, that you couldn't reason with her, because your mother's an old commie. And that's an end to it!"

"That's exactly what I'm going to tell them, you know!"

"God forbid!"

"Look, Mum, why don't you think it over some more . . . Not in terms of the present, because it's not too rosy, but in terms of the future."

"My future is up on the hill, in the cemetery. I'm looking forward to it."

"I see you're in the mood for morbid jokes."

"Oh, what am I supposed to do, Alice, if the only good things are all in the past for me?"

"I have to be off now. I think I should be wishing you a good night, shouldn't I?"

"All right, goodbye. Take care of the little'un . . . and your teeth."

So that was it: I was more of a communist than my daughter had thought.

More than even I myself had thought.

I sat down in front of the TV, but I was agitated. I couldn't keep track of what was happening on the screen. Up until my talk with Alice, I'd never thought of myself as being a communist. I'd often woken up dreaming of the nice times in my life, when I was young and worked hard, when I used to make bounteous meals for the family and we used to go on holiday, but it had never entered my head that that meant you were a communist. I missed those times, the people around me back then, the gaiety, the solidarity, but I don't know why, the word communist just didn't fit that nostalgia. In fact, I might know why. Maybe because back then, among ourselves, we used to call people communists when they gave po-faced speeches at long, boring meetings. Those who stuck to the Party line, without looking right or left, without caring about other people and without understanding individual cases. To us, it wasn't the Party members who were communists, but the political instructors and the fanatics. I don't miss them. Now, the communists were the ones who lied, who confiscated, who threw people into jail and tortured them, and did all kinds of other things. I was neither the one nor the other. What kind of communist was I? If those were the communists, then did it mean I wanted communism without communists? But was communism possible without "that kind" of communist? If not, then did I still want communism? If only they were communists, then I didn't want to be a communist. I didn't want to be, but I was. Is it possible to be something without your wanting to be?

I fell asleep in front of the TV.

I woke up confused in the middle of the night. I turned off the TV, drank some water, and went to bed. I didn't bother taking my clothes off.

The next morning, a Monday, I woke up unusually late. When I opened my eyes, some kid was shouting outside:

"Hey, you, don't be such a commie, give me a turn on the bicycle!"

I gave a crooked smile.

8

IT'S AFTERNOON. MOTHER is boiling the pig's feed on the stove: potatoes, chunks of pumpkin, bran and water. With a handful of salt. The moist seeds with their brick-red fringes are laid out on a newspaper in the sun. I'm sulking on a stool. Yesterday another chick disappeared and Mother handed Puchi over to Mister Culiță. Puchi is our old tomcat. Not even Mother knows how long she's had him. He's been old ever since I can remember. He's missing one eye and his ears are tattered. Puchi was a good cat in his day, but since he got old, he's been attacking the chicks. He doesn't have the legs to leap after mice and sparrows anymore. In the good old days, he even used to catch rats. They first tried to get rid of Puchi three years ago. It was after they got Tărcățel, the young tomcat. Wanting to get rid of him, Father put Puchi in an old bag, sewed up the neck with some wire, and went all the way to the pond, where he threw it in the water. Among the reeds. Then he went to have a talk with the forester, popped into the shop to buy some hinges, and didn't get home till evening. Puchi was in the yard, stretched out under the fence. When Father came through the gate, Puchi got up, went over to him and started rubbing himself up against his legs. Father made the sign of the cross in amazement and said the tomcat was the Devil himself, nothing less. For a while no more chicks disappeared. It looked like Puchi had got the message. The second time, a year and a half later, things were even nastier for Puchi. They asked Mister Andrei to take him into town and leave him by the station somewhere . . . No sooner said than done. I cried my eyes out. Mister Andrei told us how he had put him inside a freight car and said: "Adios, no-good tomcat!" Puchi came back two months later. Thin, frightened, limping, his fur matted. Father muttered something about him being unholy, but he left him alone. I fed him in secret and told him a thousand times not to attack the chicks because he'd get into trouble again. I taught him well. Puchi avoided everybody except me. Sanda has always liked Tărcățel. I can't stand him and I kick him up the backside whenever I get the chance. Using a rag to grasp the handle, Mother takes the cauldron off the stove and puts it on the ground to let it cool. The pig's feed smells enticing. And now they've handed Puchi over to Mister Culiță.

"If he doesn't come back in two months, I'll give you half a liter of raki," Mother promises him.

"Two months? Not even in a hundred years, I'm telling you!" he answers with a titter.

"We'll see . . ."

"You can give me half now."

"Oh no you don't. I said two months!"

"I'll die of thirst by then."

I sit sulking and wonder whether Puchi will manage to make it back again. I hope that he's an enchanted tomcat, who can turn three somersaults and transform himself into whatever he likes. Mister Culiță has got the reputation of being feeble-minded. It's going to be really hard for the poor tomcat. If he transforms himself into a bottle of raki, Culiță will drink him like water. Better he turn himself into a grain of wheat. But what if the birds peck him up? Better a poppy seed . . . The hens are hanging around the cauldron. One of the braver ones snatches a morsel of potato, but straightaway lets it go. It's probably scalding. Now I feel hungry too. The other hens immediately gather around and tug at the bit of potato. They're squabbling over it. Sometimes those hens are so cheeky that they go into the pig's sty and steal his food. They're real bandits!

"Are you coming?" shouts Sanda.

"Where?"

"To have some potatoes."

Sanda already has a stick in her hand. She shoos away the hens and starts fishing around in the cauldron. She's looking for whole potatoes, still in their skins. We wipe off the bran and peel off the skin. Mmm, they're really tasty! If Costicuţă were here, he'd eat some of the pumpkin. Yuk! It makes us feel sick just looking at it. He says it's very tasty, but I never believe him. He can tell me till he's blue in the face, but I still won't believe him. He's just trying to show off. I know that for a fact.

"Get out of there, you hens! You'll make my pig go hungry," shouts Mother.

At us, not the hens.

At the corner of the road a car appears. The dust gets whipped into the air like before a storm. The geese flap their wings and take shelter by the fence. Thrusting her chest forward and her rump back, Mother peers into the distance, sheltering her eyes with her hand.

"That's Andrei's car! How about that!"

And so it is. It comes to a stop in front of our house, by the well. Getting out of the car, Andrei waves at us. He's always happy to visit us. Auntie Lucreţia pokes her head out of the car. She's wearing sunglasses and lots of lipstick.

"Look, there's Lucreţia, too! Run and tell your father that Andrei's here," Mother hastily commands.

"Why can't Sanda go? Why me?"

I don't want to miss the excitement of greeting them and I especially don't want to miss hugging Auntie Lucreţia. She smells so nice!

"Sanda, be nice and go and tell him. That sister of yours is like a tethered goat."

But there's no need. Father appears from around the corner of the house. He probably heard the rumbling of the car. Since less than two cars pass our house in a week, he came out to see what's going on. Mother wipes her hands on her apron. That's a sign she's finished with her chores and is going to entertain her guests. Whenever Uncle Andrei comes, she always abandons everything she is doing. And especially if Auntie Lucreţia comes too. An ordinary day is transformed into a kind of celebration. We children are the happiest of all. We get out of our chores. How good it is when somebody comes from town! Uncle Andrei takes loaves of bread, sugar and cooking oil out of the trunk. Auntie Lucreţia produces two big bars of chocolate out of her handbag. Mother confiscates them on the spot and tells us we'll get them back after we've eaten. I look at Auntie Lucreţia imploringly, hoping she will intervene, but she dabs her brow with a handkerchief.

We all go and sit in the shade, apart from Mother.

"Wife, wring a chicken so that these folk can see how good our grain is!"

The adults are talking among themselves. I'm sitting next to Auntie Lucreţia so I can sniff her. You'd think I was a dog. I peek in her handbag to see whether she has any nail varnish. I ask to try on her sunglasses. The sun is blue. My hand is blue. Everything is blue. Even the ants are blue, I say to myself in amazement.

"Maybe you've got things to do . . . We can sit here by ourselves," says Uncle Andrei.

"Oho-ho, the chores are never-ending around here. You could die and there'd still be something that needed doing," answers Father.

Sanda has gone back to the cauldron. Frowning, she fishes inside. She puts the stick down and sets to work with her little hands.

"I see you've made a fair amount of briquettes this year," observes Uncle Andrei.

"That we have."

"Maybe I'll be able to send you some coal . . ."

"If you can."

Sanda comes back with two potatoes, the best ones she could find. One for Uncle Andrei and one for Auntie Lucreţia.

"What are those things sticking to it?" asks Auntie Lucreţia.

"Bran," says Uncle Andrei.

"Ugh, bran?"

"Yes, they're from the pig's feed, aren't they, Sanda?"

Sanda points at the cauldron. Lucreţia makes a face of disgust and puts the potato on the table. She wipes her fingertips with a paper napkin from her handbag. With the corner of the napkin, she cleans under her nails.

"What's wrong with it? It's clean . . . It's very good!" says Uncle Andrei, eating his with an appetite. "You wouldn't have any salt, would you?"

I look at the potato on the table, my mouth watering. But I wouldn't eat it for anything in the world.

In the end, Father eats it.

"If you make my pig go hungry, I'll give you what for!"

Uncle Andrei claps his palm to his forehead.

"Fie, I forgot!"

"What is it, Andrei? What happened?" asks Auntie Lucreţia.

Uncle Andrei has gone to the car. He takes a hat from the back seat.

"My hat!" I exclaim, leaping up.

And I run over to him.

"It's the exact same one I lost in the wagon," I rejoice.

"Exactly like it," says Auntie Lucreţia with a smile.

"Except the edge was a bit frayed," I go on. "This one's new!"

"Look closer!"

"This one's a bit frayed too," I say, puzzled. "Is it the same one?"

"The exact same one!" Auntie Lucreţia says and bursts out laughing.

"Yes, but . . . How so?"

"I found it in the wagon of seed grain," says Uncle Andrei, explaining the mystery.

"Did the Russians send it back?" asks Father.

"No, they didn't even open the wagon, the swine. They just changed the seal."

"It's about time you went off and played, kids," says Father.

"You're right . . ." I hear Uncle Andrei mutter.

And I run as fast as I can to show Mother my hat.

•

The adults are drinking beer and Sanda and I are playing. Mother goes to check the pans on the stove from time to time. The big mat under the plum tree is the house. It has two rooms. It's a country house, so it doesn't have a bathroom. It has an outside toilet in other words. Sanda wants us to play mother and child. The child gets up to mischief and the mother keeps scolding her. The child has to cry. Sanda always wants to be the mother, to scold me, even though I'm older. I have to bawl at the top of my lungs. But I like tidying up the house better. A large flat stone is the table, and the little pebbles are the chairs. We make an icon from a bit of wire and hang it from the trunk of the plum tree. That's where the corner of the house is. We don't have a mirror, but I don't want to bring the mirror from my secret apartment. And anyway, it's a country house, and so you don't really need a mirror. Sanda insists that we bring Tărcăţel, so that we'll have a cat in the house, but I won't let her. I make a cat from some wood shavings. I make it so it looks like it's resting its head on its paws. In other words, it's a sleeping cat. For furniture we need some corncobs. I go to the stove to pick a few. They have to be straight and nice, not puny ones. Mother and Auntie Lucreţia are talking. Mother tastes the food and adds some salt.

"Mica was very hardworking, she's a very helpful little girl," says Auntie Lucreţia.

I prick up my ears. I'm Mica.

"Hmm . . ."

"How many days did she stay with us? Ten, wasn't it?"

"Was it? I can't remember . . ."

"Look, here's the money for ten days. Is that enough?"

"It's enough, it's enough . . . Anyway, you shouldn't . . ."

Tears well up in my eyes. I take the corncobs and run away.

"You naughty girl! I haven't even begun to scold you and you're crying already!" says my sister.

It's evening. The meal is laid out at the back of the house. We always eat very late, after nightfall, when you can't do any more

work. The lamp is hanging from a nail in the wall, but the moon-
light is stronger. It's getting chilly, and so Auntie Lucreţia has
wrapped a shawl around her shoulders. We're having chicken
and cream.

"There's also curds and salt cheese for whoever wants them,"
announces Mother.

Tărcăţel is rubbing himself up against the legs of the tables,
the chairs, the people.

I can hardly wait to give him a kick up the backside.

Uncle Andrei helps to bring out the plates, on the condition
that he gets to eat the crispy crust left by the maize porridge
inside the cauldron. If people are getting special treats, then
Sanda and I want melted cheese and maize porridge.

"Melted cheese! Melted cheese!" we both chant.

"Not until after the chicken and cream," Mother warns us.

She pours out the maize porridge. It's a huge one. Mother
takes a piece of string and cuts it into large chunks. It cools more
quickly like that. We can hear the crickets. Tărcăţel comes within
range and whack! I don't spare him.

We eat.

"Sometimes it's nice in the country," says Auntie Lucreţia,
apropos of nothing.

"Except that there's a lot of work," says Mother with a weary
voice.

We hear a strange noise. Somebody is rattling the gate. Then
comes a shout:

"Missus Catincă! Missus Catincă!"

"Go and see who it is," Mother orders Father.

"It's you he's shouting after, not me!"

"Be off with you, enough of your jokes . . ."

Father gets up and goes around the corner of the house.
Whispering. He comes back with Mister Culiţă.

"He's says he's got business with you . . ."

"Enjoy your meal! I'm sorry, but I came for the raki, Missus
Catincă."

"Didn't I tell you to come in two months?"

"Oho-ho, he'll not be coming back in a thousand years . . . I fixed him," says Mister Culiță and starts laughing hoarsely, delighted at his handiwork.

"Two . . ."

But Mister Culiță has lifted his hand level with his eyes, to the light, holding the bloody head of Puchi. Auntie Lucreția screams in fright. Sanda and I start bawling.

9

So, I'm telling you, man, one day the Most Beloved Son of the Nation was bored to death. He was sick to the back teeth of meetings, he was bored of playing cards, he couldn't be bothered to go on any working visits . . . And he wasn't too keen on going abroad on a state visit, because his hosts were always dragging him around museums and war memorials, always giving him snails, octopuses and other scummy stuff to eat, always taking him to the opera, like in Italy, where some fat lady comrades, instead of doing the housework, would yell at the top of their voices, loud enough to burst your eardrums. And besides, he also had to talk foreign languages and his hands ached from all that conversing. After making a fool of himself in Spain, he didn't want to have anything to do with those stuck-up westerners for a while. He felt more comfortable in Africa. At least the dances they do there look more like ours, and their coconuts are a bit like pumpkins, except they grow in trees. That's where he felt at home! In fact, it had been Bobu who was to blame for the screw-up in Spain. Bobu's mind is as radiant as a dead light bulb. It was him who came up with the unfortunate idea. That is, the idea of writing what to say on the back of the Beloved Son of the Nation's necktie, in case he forgot, so that he'd have the words handy. And so he went to Spain without a care, brimming with confidence. He got off the plane and the guard of honor saluted him:

"*Buenos días, presidente!*"

"*Buenos días—*" he takes a quick look at the back of his necktie "—polyester!"

He didn't want to show his face outside the country, not for a while at least.

In any event, for that business in Spain, he gave Bobu such a thrashing at cards that it set his ears ringing. He punished him harshly: he made him stand on the desk of the Council of Ministers and shout "cuckoo!" three times, made him drink three large glasses of water one after the other just before the official meeting with Mitterand, made him dance on top of a chair to a song from the Revolution, and all kinds of other high jinks. Most of all he would have liked to watch Bobu climb the Eiffel Tower on just one leg, but there was no time to lose.

Lord, how bored he was!

When he was little and used to stomp around complaining he was bored, his father always used to tell him: hold onto your bottom and hoist yourself up in the air. Back then, he never tried it, but right now the idea appealed to him. What would it feel like to hold onto your bottom and hoist yourself up in the air? Would it cure your boredom? If he hadn't been in his office at the Central Committee of the Romanian Communist Party, and if he hadn't had such a big belly, then he'd probably have tried it, but as it was . . .

And as he sat there bored out of his mind, the Most Beloved Son of the Nation got a brilliant idea: he would go fishing. He hadn't done that since he was a mischievous young boy, when he used to go fishing with the other boys from the village, who didn't let him touch their rods except to fix the worms on their hooks. He didn't fish because he didn't have a rod, his folks were miserly, but at least he could say he had gone fishing. At least he knew how it was done, didn't he? And so straightaway he started looking around the Central Committee for a fishing rod, he climbed into a beat-up old Dacia, and off he went. He stopped at the first pond he came to. He fixed the worm on the hook, since he was an expert at doing that, he cast the bait, and the float sank. "What luck," said he. But what he pulled out was a Russian boot. Buggeration! He flung the boot aside and cast again. This time he fished out one of those billboards that had been going up

everywhere since rationing started: "Eat fish for every meal!" He
wasn't happy about it, but he had no choice: he tried a third
time. Nothing. Silence. The float was motionless. All of a sudden
plop! it sank. He tugged with all his might and what did he see?
On the hook gleamed the Golden Fish from the fairy tale, so
dazzling that it scorched your eyes. The Golden Fish wriggled
and called out:

"Don't kill me, please! Don't kill me, Most Beloved Son of
the Nation, Genius of the Carpathians! If you don't kill me, I'll
grant you a wish."

Uncle Nick gawped in amazement. Although he'd heard of
the Golden Fish, all his life he had thought it was just stuff and
nonsense. Bedtime stories for the kiddies. But now he saw it with
his own two eyes, flopping about on the grass.

As soon as he came to his senses, he said:

"What, you wretched f-f-fish, just a single w-w-wish! Even
an idiot knows you get three w-w-wishes!"

"Yes, I know, Most Beloved Son of the Nation, but we've got
problems of our own. Try to understand. Inflation . . .
Unemployment . . . Cutbacks . . . We've got our own foreign
debts to pay off . . . It's so that we won't be at the capitalists' beck
and call anymore . . . It's hard, I'm telling you! We're on an economy drive!"

The Genius of the Carpathians thinks about it . . . He thinks
and he thinks, until the veins in his temples start throbbing.
What should he ask for? To be rich? He had a whole country at
his disposal . . . To be handsome? He was handsome already . . .
To be clever? How could he be any cleverer? For the country to
achieve communism? There was no need of that: Romania was
on the right track already. To find out what it was that killed
Dej? What good would that do him? In the end he decided: he
wanted to find out what people thought of him, what life was
like in Romania, but for real, not the fairy stories the secret services told him every morning. The Golden Fish gave him an
enchanted potion, which would transform him into a fly after
he drank it. But he had to be careful, because he would turn back
into a man after nightfall.

And now wait a minute while I have a swig of this beer, because my throat's dry.

What a wag he is, that Mister Mitu!

10

LORD, HOW GOOD we had it under communism!
If I had just half of what I had back then, I'd be content.
Not even half, but a quarter, and I'd still say thank you kindly.
I had everything I could wish for. True, back then you didn't
wish for much. I don't know why, but you didn't wish for much.
I think that back then you didn't know money could do so
many things, unlike now. But relative to that world, I had everything my heart desired. I used to drink nothing but ground
coffee and instant . . . Back then coffee was hard to come by, but
it wasn't a problem for me. I had jeans when they cost eight hundred lei a pair. Eight hundred lei was a large sum, no joke! And
you couldn't find jeans just anywhere . . . But even so, I had
jeans! When I went out wearing them, the whole neighborhood
turned their heads to look. Not to mention Kent and BT cigarettes for doctors' bribes. I always had a few packets in the house,
just in case—God forbid!—I came down with some illness or I
needed a doctor's note to get sick leave. I even used to smoke
good brands of cigarettes like those, in the days when I used to
pretend, because I never inhaled.
What didn't I have!
The foreman used to bring us crates of Pepsi from the Party
restaurant. And sweets to hang from the Christmas tree. You'd
never catch me at Christmas without a tree full of sweets or without oranges. Meat, eggs, cheese, oho, if I'd been able to eat all
the stuff I could have got! When the foreman didn't bring them,
I used to go and visit the women I knew who worked in the
shops, and I never left empty-handed. Obviously, I had to give

them something in return, because they had to make a living too. Sometimes the women from the shops used to phone me to come and see them because they'd put something aside for me. They knew I'd do right by them. Not only did I used to give them baksheesh every time, but when they needed a connection somewhere, they knew I'd be able to solve it for them. To be honest, sometimes I didn't even need the things they put aside for me, but I still went to collect them. I used to take them to my folks in the country. Sometimes I took them to work or to Mrs. Rozalia, the seamstress from our block of flats. Back then I had enough stuff to give others, but now I don't even have enough for myself. And Alice is amazed that I want to vote for the ex-communists . . .

I had everything my heart desired.

If I felt like a drop of the hard stuff, I didn't poison myself with rotgut: I used to buy fine brandy, Vasconi or Unirea, or Russian vodka, the stuff that was twenty-five lei a bottle. I used to buy nothing but Guban shoes, made of soft leather that didn't give you blisters even if you walked hundreds of kilometers. I used to wash with Fa and Rexona soap, which I bought from the Poles who used to come in those little toy cars of theirs. Not to mention that Țucu had his own connections. He knew a Mr. Fane, who brought him the moon and stars if he asked. I didn't like him, because he was a bit of a spiv, I mean, he'd bring you what you wanted, but he left you out of pocket. But there was another guy, Muraru, who used to bring us strawberries and tomatoes by the crate, at half the price, or even a quarter of the price, depending on how much of a hurry he was in to get to the pub. He worked at a collective farm somewhere, near the town, and he sold everything he could lay his hands on. I don't even know when he found the time to work, because he was always driving back and forth to sell the stuff he pilfered. We got cucumbers, onions, garlic, and red peppers from him. Another guy, Mr. Sorry, was a driver at the milk factory, or rather he went around collecting the milk from the villages. Me and my husband used to call him that because every other word he said was "sorry." He couldn't say: "I ate some cherries yesterday," but he'd say: "I ate some, sorry, cherries yesterday," as if he'd eaten something shameful. We used to buy butter from him. But Mr. Sorry used to bring rich yellow butter, the likes of which you couldn't find in any of the communist shops. It was so thick you could have fired it from a gun. It didn't come in packets, but loose, in a bag. "Where does he find butter like that?" I used to ask my husband. We presumed it must be for export. I gave it to other people to taste and they'd never eaten anything so good, and so we weren't exaggerating. We tried to get the secret out of him a few times, but he was tight-lipped was Mr. Sorry; you couldn't get a word out of him. He wasn't one of those people who are ten a penny. We'd take him aside, we'd tire him out, like when you're trying to reel in a big fish, but just when we were about to get him in the net, he'd say: "Professional secret, sorry!" Until one day our Mr. Sorry turned up rather tipsy. We invited him into the kitchen to take the load off his feet and gave him something to eat and drink. I remember I gave him some whiskey, I don't know where we'd got it, but he made eyes as big as saucers and said: "This is quality stuff, sorry!" We chatted about this and that, and just when we were least expecting, Mr. Sorry started telling us what we'd been striving to get out of him for the last two years:

"Not even our director eats such good butter," he said and poured himself another tot.

And what do you think that driver of ours used to do? After loading his milk tank in some godforsaken village, he'd put three or four tennis balls inside. Then he'd drive for fifty or sixty kilometers, shaking up the milk inside the tank, like a centrifuge, and the butter would collect around the tennis balls, the cream of the cream. If the village wasn't so far away, he'd put in more tennis balls. When he arrived, all he had to do was to take out the lumps of butter, extract the tennis balls and wash them in warm water. After he let that slip, we didn't buy butter from him anymore. Truth to tell, it made me feel sick. I'd rather buy butter from the shops.

How good we had it under communism!

What, did Alice used to chew that gum that turned to pow-
der in your mouth? No way. We used to get her that Hungarian
gum which came in different flavors. She could even blow bub-
bles with it. We had as much chocolate as we liked, especially
the Chinese stuff, from the Party canteen. Biscuits, sweets,
wafers—by the cartload! We used to eat oranges by the ton . . .
And dates . . . And lemons . . . And figs . . . And bana- . . . In
fact no, I can't tell a lie: we never ate bananas. They were hard
to find. I think they were just for the bigwigs. On the other
hand, we had banana-flavored toothpaste, and so we knew what
they tasted like.

We had everything . . .

There wasn't a Sunday when we didn't go to the restaurant.
A steak used to cost ten lei. I remember it perfectly. They were
big enough to feed two people. A beer cost three lei. Or five lei,
if it was the really good stuff. A Pepsi was three lei too. Sparkling
wine was eighteen lei. From the food shop, with the deposit on
the bottle, it cost twenty-one lei. A packet of Kent also cost eighteen lei. I remember all the prices. That's when we had the best
life. Lord, what a meal you could eat at the restaurant for a hundred lei! Including dessert. Back then I used to earn four or five
thousand lei, depending on the month and on results. Lord,
what a lot of money that was! Now, what with inflation, a tram
ticket costs five thousand lei. I don't even want to think about
what a steak costs! I know, wages are higher, but it still doesn't
compare. When I see the prices nowadays, I feel like I'm on a
different planet. Prices with lots of noughts, as long as caterpillars. Under communism, a nought was worth something, but
nowadays it's worth nothing. Four of today's noughts are not
even worth one nought from Ceaușescu's day.

We bought a cooker as soon as we were allocated a flat. Two
thousand lei we paid for it. We didn't get a washing machine
until later, because I've always liked to wash by hand. When
I've scrubbed something myself, I know it's clean. I got a washing machine mainly because Țucu kept nagging me about it,
but once I had one, I saw it was useful. We lacked for nothing.
We even had a television. We put our names on the list at the

shop and six months later they phoned us to tell us our turn had come. As easy as pie. We paid it off in installments. It was a black-and-white television and it lasted us twenty years. The communists built things to last, not like nowadays: I bought a pair of shoes from the market recently, and the sole peeled off three days later. After ten years, we converted our black-and-white TV into a colored one, because that was the fashion. We'd seen other people doing it. You got a piece of colored glass and fitted it in a wooden frame in front of the screen. We had a pane of green glass and it made everything different shades of green. Then, Alice visited a friend from school, I think it was when she was in her second or third year, she saw a blue screen and pestered us until we found some blue glass. You changed the color whenever you felt like it. Real color TVs appeared later. They were Russian. We got one even before the Revolution. We waited a year to get it, but that was only because we had a connection who wangled us a place nearer the top of the list. What can I say? We had everything! It was good . . .

And how we traveled!

We went all over the country . . . On our holidays, we used to go to the seaside, to the mountains, and once we even went to the Danube Delta. We also used to visit my godparents and cousins. Because you couldn't go abroad . . . Not that you would have had the time, because by the time you'd been to the seaside and the mountains, once you'd visited your relatives, the holidays were over. When would you have had the time to go anywhere else? But even so, we still made it to Bulgaria. To Varna. It looked like Romania. What was the point of going abroad if it was the same as at home? The mountains over there are still mountains, the sand is still sand, and the sea is still water. Maybe it's not even as nice as in Romania and so you'll pay all that extra money for nothing. Just so that you can say you've been abroad. Few people have a country as beautiful as ours. I've got a plastic bag full of photographs taken on holiday. The whole country is there, inside that bag. Nowadays I can't even afford to have a photograph taken for my identity card.

There wasn't a weekend when we didn't go for a picnic, or to play volleyball, or to visit the monasteries of Bukovina. It wasn't always easy, what with the petrol rationing, but we managed. The only people who didn't manage were the ones who couldn't be bothered. Then there was that nasty period, during the economy drive, when only cars with even registration numbers were allowed on the roads one week, and only cars with odd numbers the next week. But even then we still got around. One week with our car, the next week with the neighbors' car or our workmates' car. And we still had fun. We were young and it was nice. Two years after the Revolution, we had to sell our car, because lately it was nothing but decoration. The price of petrol had gone up, and we couldn't afford it anymore. Nowadays, I couldn't even afford a pair of roller skates.

If I could go back in time to the communist period, I'd be happy. I'd be happy if I had just a quarter of what I had then, not even half.

Maybe I ought to have told Alice about all these things . . . But back then she was always studying for school. And how am I supposed to tell her all this and so much more over the phone?

11

THIS MEMORY IS very clear. I'm at Auntie Lucreția's and Uncle Andrei's and I feel awful. When I was least expecting it, the illness returned. The pain and the bleeding and the dizziness again. I kept hoping it wouldn't come back. I can barely stand up and I'm washing the dishes. I straighten my back, so I can take a deeper breath. I feel like I'm suffocating. I'm trying to behave like nothing is wrong.

I'm washing the dishes and I'm scolding God. I'm upset with Him.

Why now? Why me?

He could at least have let me enjoy these few days in town.

In the end I'll have to go to the doctor's.

I promise myself I'll do it, but I don't know how to go about it.

I promised myself once before and I didn't keep my word.

I hear footsteps . . . Someone's coming toward the kitchen.

I adopt a breezy sort of air . . .

"There are a lot of dishes, aren't there?" says Auntie Lucreția.

"I'm used to it, Auntie! At home I wash those great big cauldrons . . ."

"But what's that there? I can see a stain . . . I think your period's come . . ."

I freeze. I grasp the edge of the sink and start to sob.

"What's wrong, Mica? It's only a skirt! If it doesn't come out in the wash, I'll throw it away. It's old anyway . . ."

"Auntie . . . I have to tell you something . . . I've . . . I've got a serious illness . . . Auntie . . ."

Auntie gives me a painkiller and tactfully explains what happens to young girls' bodies as they grow up.

"Cotton wool isn't just for wiping the oil lamp, Mica! And now, go and lie down in bed if you don't feel well!"

12

AND SO HERE he is, our Uncle Nick, transformed into a great big greenish-looking fly, eyes as big as radishes, buzzing around where the whim takes him. First of all, he flies into a classroom. He lands on the portrait of himself and listens. It's a history lesson, and a jug-lugged guy is standing at the front.

"Well then, Pandele, what important event took place in our country in 1918?" asks the teacher.

"The Great Union of 1918 took place in 1918, Comrade Teacher!"

"Not bad, Pandele, but I wanted more than that from you. Please concentrate. What else happened? Something far more important . . ."

"Also in 1918 Comrade Nicolae Ceauşescu, the Secretary General of the Romanian Communist Party and President of the Socialist Republic of Romania, was born in Scorniceşti."

"That's right, Pandele! Bravo! I have just one more question for you and then you can sit back down . . . What important event took place in 1848?"

Pandele looks stumped. You can see from his face that he doesn't have a clue. He's wringing his fingers. "Come on," buzzes the fly in encouragement, "it's easy!" Finally, the guy opens his mouth to speak:

"Well, in 1848, they, er . . . they celebrated the sixtieth anniversary of the birth of Comrade Nicolae Ceauşescu, the Secretary General of the Romanian Communist Party and President of the Socialist Republic of Romania."

Well versed as he was, Uncle Nick had never thought of

anything like that. "He's cut out to be a propagandist, jug-lugs there," he said to himself, determined not to lose track of him. He was right in a way: did history necessarily have to unfold only in a forward direction from his birth and his becoming head of state? Ultimately, the boy was a visionary . . . But one who'd been born too late.

He buzzed around a bit more and then flew into the next classroom. It was a sociopolitical sciences lesson, which was almost over.

"Does anybody have any questions?" asked the teacher, a lady comrade. "I can see one hand raised. Let's hear it, Viorel."

"You said that money would become obsolete under communism. How will people buy what they need if there is no money?"

"Bravo, Viorel, good question," says the teacher with a smile. "Let me give you another example, so that you'll understand better. Let's say, Viorel, that your parents need some maize flour. They won't have to go to a shop for it, instead they'll go to one huge store where each person takes as much as he needs, without having to pay. Then they'll go to the central market, where there will be a huge mound of potatoes, from which everybody will take as much as they need, depending on how many family members they have. Also without having to pay. Now do you understand?"

"I understand, comrade. But we don't much like potatoes or maize porridge . . ."

"You will like them, Viorel, you will like them! Believe me!"

Uncle Nick leaves the classroom, flapping his wings in annoyance. In the corridor, two teachers are having a cigarette and chatting.

"I say socialist democracy was born in heaven," says the first, the one wearing specs.

"How so?" says the second in amazement, the one with the beard.

"Well, when God created Eve, He showed her to Adam and said: Go on, choose!"

"Ha, ha, ha! That's a good one!"

Uncle Nick can't stand intellectuals as it is, but now he's really determined to do something about it. Elena was right when she said that people with beards and specs are enemies of the people in disguise. That they ought to be made to take some exercise, picking beetroot with their teeth and potatoes with ice cream spoons, but with a quota to meet, not just anyhow. Elena hasn't been able to stand them ever since she was a young underground activist and used to sell sunflower seeds in the train station. The intellectuals never bought her wares. They were always too stuck up. They used to buy their kids lollipops rather than supporting national sunflower seed production.

Hovering above the town like a hawk that's shrunk in the wash, he spots a great big line behind a food shop, snaking and twisting back and forth. Puzzled, he descends to see what's going on. He lands on the shoulder of the last person in the line. It's a mechanic wearing overalls, covered in grease, with a monkey wrench in his pocket. It's obvious from a mile off that he's bunking off work.

"What are we lining up for?" the mechanic asks the lady comrade in front of him.

"I don't know, I've only just got here," she says. "But whatever it is, I'm short of it."

He asks another two or three people, but nobody has a clue. The mechanic goes all the way to the front of the line. The first person in the line is a pale old man, with eyes sunk deep in their sockets, with livid hands clutching a trembling cane.

"Say, granddad, what goods have they got?"

"Nothing at the moment, sonny."

"Have you been waiting long, granddad?"

"Oh, yes, since this morning. I was walking along slowly and all of a sudden I started to feel dizzy, so I leaned up against this door until I felt better . . . I don't know how long I've been leaning here, maybe a quarter of an hour, maybe longer . . . But when I came to my senses, there was already this big line behind me . . ."

"What if they aren't going to receive any goods, granddad? Are we waiting for nothing?"

"Maybe the good Lord will bring some goods . . . I don't feel like going home now, sonny, since I've never been the first person in a line this long . . ."

Uncle Nick would have really liked to give them a surprise, to supply the shop with some top-quality meat or bananas like they'd never dreamed of, but then he realized that as a fly he didn't have any power. He resigned himself and quickly landed on the plastic bag of a woman who was just going into the shop over the road.

"Excuse me, have you got any fish?" asks the woman.

"No, here we don't have meat, it's the shop next door that doesn't have fish," the woman behind the counter answers politely.

"So that's the way it is," mutters the fly. Every morning they reported to him that the shelves of the shops were groaning under the weight of all the good things, all the meat and milk, that the populace was gurgling like a contented baby, that the corncobs were as big as policemen's truncheons and the potatoes as big as footballs, that everybody was laughing, dancing, laboring away. "I'll be having words with you, Avramescu!" he says to himself and flies away.

He arrives in a park, where he's drawn by the sound of young people laughing. "So there are happy people in this country after all," rejoices Uncle Nick. He puts on a spurt and flies up to a group of high-school students, gathered around a park bench. They're smoking and passing around a bottle of booze.

"Let me tell you a good one . . . So, one fine day Vladimir Ilich Lenin dies. As bold as brass, he goes straight up to the pearly gates. When Saint Peter sees him, he almost has a heart attack. 'What are you doing here, you mangy dog? Go on, get lost, your place is down where they all wear horns.' Fuming, Lenin slings his hook and goes down to the realm of the Evil One. After a while, Saint Peter bumps into the wee devil who fetches the firewood for the cauldrons of pitch. 'How are things, you wee devil?' asks Saint Peter. 'First of all, it's comrade wee devil to you,' said he, all sniffy. 'And besides, you ought to know that God doesn't exist and so take care, because the proletarian revolution will be starting any moment.'"

"Ha, ha, ha! Do you know why Comrade Andropov died?"

"No!" cry the others in unison.

"Neither do I, but during the autopsy he couldn't keep still . . ."

"But do you know why Comrade Khrushchev killed his cat?"

"No!"

"Because instead of miaow, it kept saying Mao-o-o-o!"

"Ha, ha, ha!"

"That's a good one! But wait a minute, let me tell you another one from the same series. So, a listener phones in to the radio: Excuse me, is it possible for a woman to give birth three times in the same calendar year? The presenter answers: No, Comrade Nicolae Ceauşescu, no, it isn't."

"Ha, ha, ha!"

"Wait, let me tell you another . . ."

"Go on then, get on with it!"

"Apparently, the tap dance was invented by a member of the working class, Stepan Stepanovich Stepanov, who had ten children but only one chamber pot!"

"Weak!"

"That one gets a D!"

"Let me tell you another, this one gets an A minus! So, the Comrade and Mrs. Comrade are invited on a state visit to France. After they've finished with all the official meetings, Mrs. Comrade insists they visit the Louvre. In front of a painting, Elena gets all excited and cries out: 'Wow, what a great Da Vinci!' The guide discreetly whispers to her: 'It looks a bit like a Da Vinci, but it's a Rembrandt, madam.' Mrs. Comrade walks another few paces and then she exclaims: 'Phew, what a wonderful Utrillo!' The guide intervenes again: 'Allow me to make a small correction, madam: it's a Da Vinci.' She goes into the next room and says: 'This one I know! I know for a fact it's Grigorescu's *Gypsy Woman*!' The guide smiles to himself: 'I'm sorry to disappoint you, madam, but that is a mirror.'"

They all burst out laughing.

"But do you know what the seven wonders of communism are?"

"No!" they cry in unison.

"One: in Romania everybody has a job. Two: although everybody has a job, nobody works. Three: although nobody works, the production exceeds one hundred per cent of the target. Four: although the target is exceeded by more than one hundred per cent, the shops are empty. Five: although the shops are empty, everybody has food to eat. Six: although everybody has food to eat, nobody is satisfied. Seven: although nobody is satisfied, everybody applauds."

Furious, Uncle Nick flies away as fast as he can. He doesn't want to hear any more. The ingrates! He built them kindergartens and schools, he provided them with hours and hours of political instruction and patriotic labor—what more did they want? He made them Hawks of the Homeland and Pioneers, he allowed them to sing patriotic anthems, he never stopped them from joining the 23 August Liberation Day parade, he gave them two hours of television a day—what more did they want? He even allowed them to visit Bulgaria and the Soviet Union, to take part in the Song of Romania spectacular—what more did they want? He even allowed them to paint his portrait. Ingrates.

Tired and angry, he lands—hard to break the habits of a fly—on a turd. Before long he hears voices. He looks around, but can't see anybody. Curious, he eavesdrops.

"Dad, is it true that you can live inside a plum?"

"It's true, son!"

"What about inside an apple?"

"Inside an apple, too, son."

"Don't tell me you can also live inside a banana too! Yum!"

"Of course you can, son, why not?"

"So why do we live inside this stinky turd?"

"Well, son, there's nothing we can do about that. It's our country, and so we've got to be proud of it, my boy!"

Frightened to death, the Most Beloved Son of the Nation speeds off to the Central Committee. There's nowhere he feels safer than there. And if he ever catches a golden fish again, instead of going through the same ordeal, he'll melt it down and make it into a gold tap for the House of the People.

What a wag he is, that Mister Mitu!

13

As I was saying, on Monday I woke up out of sorts. I puttered around the house, not doing much. I made some soup, did a little cleaning. When I'm on my own, I eat very little. At one point, I wanted to go to church to light a candle and pray, but I felt too tired. At lunchtime a nephew phoned, asking for a favor. A friend of his, a journalist, wanted to do an article on nostalgia for communism, and he, Cătălin, thought that I might be able to lend him a hand.

"What's this, Cătălin, you pick me to put in the paper?"

"Come on, Auntie, it's for a friend . . ."

"But am I really the right person?"

"Well, Dad said that you miss Ceaușescu, that you were a Party member and that you had it good, and so I thought that . . ."

So, it's not only Alice who thinks I'm a commie.

I told him to come by on Wednesday morning.

It's true: I had been a Party member. That doesn't mean that come December '89 I wasn't shouting "Down with Ceaușescu!" or that I wasn't on the edge of my seat when I watched him and his wife being executed on television. It doesn't mean that I didn't feel sorry afterward because they'd shot him on Christmas Day, without giving him a chance to defend himself. It doesn't mean that I didn't miss the life I'd led, but without going to lay flowers on their grave.

I was made a Party member almost a year before the regime fell. I didn't join; I was made a member without having to lift a finger. One fine day, the Party secretary at the factory discovered that there were too few women members. The number was below some percentage or other. It was all Elena Ceaușescu's doing: she was fighting to increase the number of women in the Party and in leadership positions and she had set a minimum quota, which was compulsory. As the factory where I worked was all about hard toil with sheet metal and rusty iron, with lathes, grinders and hole-punching machines, there weren't many lady comrades. And so the Party secretary was desperate for recruits; he would even have invited you to the cinema just to get you to join. Not that he cared about the Party; he was just looking after his own cushy job. "Looking after" is an understatement: he clung to it tooth and nail. That's because folk like that, once you took them out of a management position, were incapable of doing anything else. They'd forgotten everything they ever learned, if they'd ever done a trade. They could no longer tell a nut from a bolt. And so our man was running around trying to get his percentage up, because otherwise he'd have been out on his ear. It was no joking matter. So, there weren't very many women at the factory to start with, but to join the Party you still had to meet a number of conditions. You couldn't have any disciplinary infringements. Your relatives couldn't have any criminal convictions, and such-like. You had to have healthy origins, in other words, your parents had to be working class or peasants, but that no longer mattered, they weren't fussy anymore: the children of intellectuals were good enough, as long as they got the numbers up. I met all the conditions, and so the great big Party secretary himself turned up at my workplace, as jolly as could be, and invited me to submit my file. Mind you, he didn't summon me to his office, but came looking for me in person, although otherwise you never saw him on the factory floor except during inspections . . . Of course, I didn't realize that until later, after I'd boned up on the Party's internal regulations. After that, I was amazed that such a bigwig had come looking for me. He was all smiles, he kept calling me comrade, saying what an honor it was, how it was evidence of trust, and blah, blah. I wasn't against it, but nor was I very proud of it, and so I didn't give him a definite answer. I didn't like the fact that I'd have to go to lots of meetings, like the other members did. Just as we would be about to go home, they would get roped into a Party meeting. I never thought about the fact that it was a criminal party, as they say nowadays, that they put people in prison and starved the population. I don't know why, but that never crossed my mind for one moment. Maybe it was because I never had any relatives who were in prison, maybe it was because I was nonetheless content with the life I led. I say "nonetheless" because there were unpleasant parts. But I'm much more content now with the life I led then than I was at the time. Because now I can make the comparison. I'm not saying that if things got worse in the future I'd miss the life I lead right now . . . Not long afterward, the foreman came to have a word with me. He said I should agree, that I had nothing to lose. That if I wanted to train to be a foreman, it was almost compulsory to be a Party member. I never did train to be a foreman, but I did sign up. I couldn't refuse the foreman. He had a way of treating us that meant it was difficult ever to turn him down. I submitted my file and in a very short time I was holding my red Party member's card. In the main, I began to go to meetings and to pay my dues. It wasn't until later that I found out there were benefits too. I had priority over the others when it came to choosing the weeks I would go on holiday: "The comrade is a Party member!" It counted. We went to the best resorts with the best hotels at the lowest prices. Sometimes it was even free. It counted when it came to promotions. I already had a gas cylinder and a flat, but they depended on your political situation too. In fact, when I was at night school, I'd seen that the teachers were more attentive to the Party members, more indulgent in other words. Of course, there was no written rule that the teachers had to be like that, but that's what happened. Probably they were thinking that one of those students might go on to become a bigwig and cause them problems. Or maybe they just wanted to make some useful connections. What I mean is that besides the official benefits, there were lots of other situations where it was an advantage to be a Party member. Even the police, when they asked for your identity papers on the street, looked at you differently if you also produced a red Party member's card. It wasn't a matter of respect, but rather fear: maybe you were a bigwig and could make them lose their jobs. Whereas if you weren't a Party member, you couldn't possibly have an important job, and so they treated you with contempt. In the end, I wasn't sorry that I'd joined, even if I didn't make much of a career out of it. A boy from my village, who was hopeless at school, went on to study at the Party College, at the urging of his uncle, who knew what was what, and he ended up being a mayor. He was elected, obviously. But at elections, there was just one candidate, chosen by the Party. I could have done the same as him, but I wasn't tempted. You don't have to have a brilliant mind to become a Party activist. If you had healthy references and knew how to chant long live such and such, it was enough.

To tell the truth, my red card made me nervous during the Revolution. It sounds laughable now, but I was trembling in my boots at the time. After a few days of euphoria, when people set light to their membership cards and held them over their heads like torches, I started asking myself questions. What if communism comes back? That was my first fear. The Soviets were nearby: all they had to do was climb in their tanks and they'd have been here in a jiffy. The fear of the Russians has always been greater here in the north of the country. If they came and asked to inspect our membership cards, what would I do then? And so I didn't burn mine. But what if the people who had come to power started hunting down the communists? That was the second fear. If I burned my card, it was bad, but if I kept it, it was just as bad. I was confused. In the end, I said to myself that I'd better hide it. It was as if I didn't have one, but I could get it out if necessary. No sooner said than done. The least likely place anybody would search was behind the icon. I haven't looked, but I think it's still there, even now.

All Monday it was as if I was in a trance.

The conversation with Alice and Cătălin's telephone call had reawakened all kinds of memories in me. I was trying not to get swept away by them, to bring my mind back to this fourth-floor flat, but it wasn't at all easy. I tried to snap myself out of it, to laugh at myself. Come on then, you commie, sit down and watch a film on the TV if you've got nothing else to do! Get the vacuum cleaner out, wake up all the rats under the carpet! I was trying to keep myself busy but my mind kept going back, raking over the past. My parents. The village. Treading the manure to make briquettes. Auntie Lucreția and Uncle Andrei. The hostel. Țucu. Bills. Events. Words and faces. Alice. They didn't come back one by one, like sheep all in a line, but they came in a whirl, all at once. They wanted me to pay attention to them all simultaneously. As if my past were a map full of little lights all blinking at the same time, like a class of studious pupils who all raise their hands at the same time to answer the teacher's question. There was just one electric current lighting up all the bulbs and there was just one question all the pupils had to answer: was Emilia Apostoae really happy or is that just was she thinks, because she's mad?

"Yes, you were happy in your way!" each of my memories tells me.

But once the answer to that question had been wrenched out of them, yet more questions popped out, like from inside a Russian doll: how could you have been happy when others were unhappy? What did you do to make others happy? How many happy people would there have had to be around you in order for you to have the right to be happy?

That night the sky was cloudless and the stars were clear.

14

I'M ON THE bus. My heart feels like it's shrunk to the size of a pinhead. I've run away from home. I left Sanda a note telling her I've gone to Town and for her not to worry. All I've taken with me are the clothes on my back, my identity card and some money, a very small sum. I'm placing my hope in Uncle Andrei and Auntie Lucreţia. I'm seventeen and I've finished ten years of schooling in our village. If I want to enter high school, I have to go to town. I've been sounding out Mother and Father about it for the last two years, but they refuse even to discuss it. Their answer is to ask me who will stay there in their house in the village and look after them in their old age. Most of the girls my age have already left. They come back only in the holidays. I don't want to end up the village idiot. There aren't even very many boys my age in the village. They've spread out all over the country: Bucharest, Timişoara, Constanţa . . . All the young people scatter like partridges. I'M NOT THE VILLAGE IDIOT. I feel like bursting into tears. I lean my head on the seat in front and hold it in. There are other people from the village in the bus. I don't have enough money to live on if I get into high school, but I'll attend a vocational school. If so many no-hopers have been able to manage, then I'll do the same, I say to myself by way of encouragement. I'll escape by my own efforts and using my own money. I wipe my nose on the hem of my dress. I don't lift my head from the back of the seat in front, thinking my eyes must be red. I would have liked to leave with my parents' blessing, for them have seen me off at the bus station. That would have been nice. But Mother and Father don't even want to discuss it. Or to listen. THEY'LL BE SORRY ONE DAY. Auntie Lucreția has a two-year-old son, Tudor. I tell myself that I could look after him. I don't want to live with them free of charge. Or else I'll live in a hostel or something. She doesn't work at the telephone exchange anymore. She does the books at a storeroom. "They kicked her out," said Uncle Andrei, aggrieved. Because she was tired, Auntie forgot to say: "Long live the struggle for peace" or whatnot. Some Party bigwig was on the other end of the line and the very next day she had to look for another job. That's how she ended up in the storeroom at a textiles factory. "A good job they didn't expel her from the Party," said Father. Uncle Andrei nodded: "That's right."

The bus is crawling along like a worm. The metal has heated up and the smell of paint mingles with the diesel fumes. I'm starting to feel sick. It's a bumpy section of road and my stomach is bouncing up and down like a rubber ball. The dust has dried out my mouth and nostrils. I'd ask the driver to stop for me to get out and take a breath of fresh air, but everybody is looking at me. I don't want anybody to see me; I don't want anybody to talk to me. The less attention I draw to myself the better. I fix my eyes on my toes. I'm wearing a pair of white sandals, cut away at the toes. I discover that my toenails are dirty and I remember how good I was to my parents. I didn't leave before we finished making this year's manure briquettes. I didn't leave them in the lurch. Tears well up in my eyes once more. It makes me forget how sick to the stomach I'm feeling. I'm a little better now.

The bus comes to a halt. It's the edge of a village. I look to see where the stop is, but there aren't any signs anywhere. The driver climbs out. He looks lively. Although he's soaked in sweat, he's whistling a merry tune. A folk tune. He enters the gate of the house next to the bus. An old woman greets him. They talk to each other and then the driver calls to us:

"You can get off the bus to stretch your legs for a little. There's a well over there."

Nobody makes any move, as if they haven't heard what he said. As if they all want to show him that they just want to get to their destination as quickly as possible. The driver and the old woman start picking plums. Two men get off the bus and light cigarettes. A child then gets off. He starts ripping up blades of grass at the edge of the ditch.

"We're not even halfway there," somebody says.

If I don't get off, they'll all start looking at me, I say to myself.

The driver wipes a few plums on the corner of his shirt and starts eating them. He spits the seeds up in the air, amusing himself. The old woman puts the fruit in a transparent plastic bag.

I go to the well and rinse my face.

The people are livelier now. They have started chatting among themselves.

I avoid them.

Finally, the driver comes back with two bottles of milk and the bag of plums. He revs the motor. The black smoke from the exhaust pipe makes big clouds. Like storm clouds. We all jostle to board the bus.

The journey seems never-ending. The seventy kilometers keep dilating, they become a thousand. The nearer we get to town, the more frightened I become. I'm terrified that Auntie Lucreția and Uncle Andrei might not be at home. I hadn't thought of that. What if they're on holiday? What if they're at home but tomorrow they bundle me off back home? How will I be able to show my face? The shame!

On the other hand, I'M SICK OF MANURE.

I'd sooner sleep in the park than make manure briquettes.

I'm sick of mud. I don't want to marry somebody called Culiță.

I'm sick of it! Sick, sick, sick! I'm not the village idiot! No!

When Auntie Lucreția opens the door, I'm bawling my eyes out.

"Don't . . . don't send me away, Auntie, don't . . ."

"Shush! The child's asleep!"

"Don't . . . send me . . ."

"What's up with you, girl? Come in. Have I ever sent you away?"

I fall into her arms.

"What is it, Mica?"

"I've . . . I've run away from home, Auntie!"

"They sent you away?"

"No . . . no . . . I ran away."

We sit on the sofa and I tell her everything, sobbing. She holds me in her arms.

"That's enough crying. I had enough of Tudor's crying until he got off to sleep! Would you like something to eat?"

"No."

"Then let's go to bed. If you're a good girl, tomorrow we'll do our nails."

The door of the room where I'm sleeping is open. In the morning I hear voices in the kitchen. Have they come to get me? No, it's Uncle Andrei's voice. He's come back from his work trip.

"I don't know, Lucreția dear, I don't know what to say . . . It's a delicate matter. What right have I got to go against their decision?"

"If the girl wants to study, it's a shame for her to be stuck in that wretched village."

I nod in agreement.

"He's my brother, Lucreția, you understand?"

"Would you have got where you are today if you'd stayed there?"

"It's true that . . ."

"You know what? Put the blame on me. Tell them that it was me, so that you won't be stuck in the middle . . . What do you say?"

"Hmm . . ."

"Mica could look after Tudor. She's good with children . . . She already knows housekeeping . . ."

"Will you come with me to talk to them?"

I love Auntie Lucreția once more.

We're in the living room. Tudor is pushing his toy tractor. The telephone is next to the plate of cakes. The teacups are stacked up. I look at the piece of paper with the phone numbers that Auntie Lucreția has handed me. My hands are trembling.

"What are you doing? Aren't you going to phone?" she asks.

I've never talked on the phone before and I don't feel like trying now.

"Don't you want to phone, Auntie?"

"Oh, you're just like your Uncle Andrei. He always gets me to do the talking. You country folk . . . The telephone won't eat you!"

I gulp three times.

Auntie Lucreția is very good on the phone. She has a teacher's voice. I move closer to hear what they are saying on the other end of the line.

"Yes, we're interested in the textiles school."

"There aren't any more places, comrade. It's a bit too late . . ."

"None at all? Please check again. We'll make it worth your while."

"I know for a fact that there aren't any more. If you had phoned two days ago, it could have been resolved. I've sent off the files already."

"What about elsewhere?"

"The only places left are in metalworking . . . We stopped taking people yesterday, but if you come tomorrow morning, we'll try to arrange something . . ."

"Comrade, I'm looking for something suitable for a very nice and clever young lady."

She gives me a wink and I blush.

"Well, I don't know . . . For a young lady . . . There's a lot of dust and rust . . ."

"But it doesn't involve manure, does it?"

"No, comrade, no manure. That's animal husbandry."

"Aha!"

"There are other girls signed up for metalworking, you know!"

"But isn't there anything else?"

"Nothing else. It's very late, like I told you."

Auntie Lucreția gestures to me to ask whether I accept, and I vigorously nod my head.

"Very well, metalworking it is, comrade!" says Auntie Lucreția.

"Please tell me the candidate's name."

"Mica Burac."

"Emilia," I whisper.

"I'm sorry, I meant Emilia! Emilia Burac."

"I've made a note. My name is Constantin Gospodaru. Come to see me tomorrow morning and everything will be resolved. Constantin Gospodaru, don't forget!"

After she hangs up the phone, I feel like kissing her. For the umpteenth time in the last few days.

"I'll get hold of Andrei to tell him to bring something for tomorrow, because you can't go empty-handed," murmurs Auntie Lucreția.

15

We've had our break and now we're each going about our jobs. I'm making medium-sized boxes with lots of compartments for my neighbor Rozalia. The kind of thing I imagine a seamstress would need. Sanda is lending me a hand. It's been more than a year since she got a job here at the workshop. Only I know how much I had to beg the foreman to take her. I told him she's hardworking and that she doesn't talk out of turn, all the required palaver. I pestered him so relentlessly that in the end he agreed. But ultimately, she hasn't shown me up and the foreman has nothing to reproach me for. Sanda is in seventh heaven. Given her wage, I'm not surprised.

The young gatekeeper comes in, holding Alice by the hand. The little girl is crying and sobbing. I drop everything and rush over to see what's wrong. The gatekeeper tells me that the wee child came to him bawling, saying she wanted to talk to her mother. I've brought her to work two or three times, when she didn't have school and I didn't have anybody to sit with her at home, and how about that: she remembers the way. She shouldn't have come on her own, but I'll scold her later.

Sobbing, she tells me that she got eight out of ten for handwriting.

At least it's nothing more serious, I think to myself.

"How come you only got eight out of ten?" I ask.

"I don't know," she wails, "but it isn't fair . . ."

She's flushed and snotty. She looks so funny that I almost burst out laughing.

She takes out her exercise book and shows me how nice her

handwriting is. I tell her that I like it, but if the comrade teacher gave her an eight, then there must be a reason.

I know the reason, but I don't say anything.

"Laura's handwriting is a lot worse than mine and she got a ten."

Even children are able to understand certain things.

Laura is the daughter of the head of the parents' committee. The committee is mainly in charge of organizing excursions and collecting money for various occasions, but above all for International Women's Day, the end of the school year, and the teacher's birthday. At the last committee meeting there was a heated discussion. I pointed out that the presents for the teacher are getting more and more expensive every year, which doesn't seem right to me. Laura's mother said that the comrade teacher deserved it, because she works very hard with the children, she puts in a lot of effort, blah, blah, blah. That's what started the argument. Ţucu calls the teacher Madam Gold Necklace. That's because she's mad about gold jewelry. As chunky as possible. Presents from the class mean necklaces, earrings, rings. Last time, Laura's mother proposed a bracelet. But I'm convinced that the suggestion, or rather the order, came from the comrade teacher. That's why I lost my temper. I can almost picture the scene: all smiles, Laura's mother goes to the comrade teacher and tells her in that perfumed voice of hers that we, the third form collective, thank her from the bottom of our hearts for the efforts she has made and that we would like to offer her a small token of our esteem, but that we cannot decide what, there have been a number of suggestions and we don't know which is best. The teacher rolls her eyes, feigns embarrassment, says she was only doing her duty, that there is no need, but if they insist, since she's getting ready to go to a wedding anyway, a modest bracelet might be a suitable gift. Of course, she does not say "gold." Laura's mother thanks her from the bottom of her heart once more, this time for having solved our dilemma, and then she comes to the parents' committee with what looks like a random suggestion: let's all chip in and buy her, let's say, a bracelet, because we've bought her so many rings and necklaces that the poor comrade must be sick of getting the same thing.

I wipe her nose and wash her face. I try to soothe her.

In a way, I'm the one who's guilty for her tears. I always tell her not to come home with low marks. That if she gets low marks, she'll end up like her mother, bending sheets of metal in a factory. Or worse still, she'll end up cleaning public toilets.

I comfort her and explain that the comrade teacher doesn't have anything against her, but that she just has to try to write more nicely, to be well-behaved and obedient.

What else could I tell her?

I've heard that the teachers in the other forms are more reasonable: it's enough to give them a box of chocolates, a bunch of flowers, a nice bibelot, a coffee service. The one we've got is grasping. But she was the only one who had vacant places when I enrolled Alice in the first form, because places in the good teachers' classes get taken before the start of the school year and you have to have connections. Obviously, nor does Madam Gold Necklace turn down little tokens of esteem brought by individual parents, without there being any special occasion, but just so that she won't forget your child is in her class. I've been remiss on that score too. I haven't laid eyes on her since the start of term.

Sanda offers to mind Alice so that I can finish my box.

She takes her by her little hand and they go out of the workshop.

I'm working and thinking that it's a good thing in life to have nice handwriting, like I do. You're always at an advantage. Wherever you might work, there's always a need for somebody to write up the political bulletins ledger, to fill in the activities chart and other paperwork. Nobody looks at what's inside the ledgers, but it's important that the charts be clear, written in two or three different colors and in a calligraphic hand. The person who writes up all that stuff is the boss's right-hand man. It's a good thing in life to have nice handwriting, and no mistake!

•

After I finish, I go outside for a breath of fresh air.

It's spring and it's warm. The vines have started to come into leaf.

I hear chuckling to the side of the workshop and I go to see what's happening. Sanda, Alice, Mitu and Sorin are sitting on the curb and laughing infectiously. It makes me feel like laughing, even though I don't know what they're talking about. Alice points at the dogs, but I can't see anything amusing. Sanda explains, choking with laughter.

What have the rascals been up to?

We have three dogs, which mostly hang around the gate. They're for show, because not one of them bites. If you toss them a scrap of something, they're your best friends. They gave them chunks of maize porridge mixed with salt and coated in grease to make it go down more easily, and the dogs ate their fill. Not long after that, they got a raging thirst. They poured some water for them in an empty fish tin, not the ordinary water they're used to, but the sparkling stuff. Now they're watching as the poor dogs try to quench their thirst.

This must be one of Mitu's gags.

I sit down next to them. Now I know what it's all about, I burst out laughing.

There are two tins and three dogs. Bebe, the youngest one, who has thick grey fur, tries the water with the tip of his tongue and leaps backward. He looks questioningly at the other two, Anghelache and Titic, who sniff the water cautiously. The fizzing water splashes Titic on the nose and he gives his head a violent shake. He can't understand it, but his thirst impels him to try the water. Bebe, who is probably the greediest and also the thirstiest now, quickly laps up some water and starts to whine. It brought tears to his eyes. Anghelache and Titic look at him curiously, and then they go up to him and sniff him. All three go back to the tins. Alice is laughing so hard she lets slip a fart. Anghelache looks at the tin mistrustfully, with one eye. He gives it a push with his paw, as if to see whether it is alive, whether it will move. That makes the water fizz some more and so when he moves closer, in slow motion, it sprays him with invisible droplets between his eyelashes. He withdraws, blinking, but not making any sudden movements, keeping an eye on his quarry. Bebe is the most impatient. He laps some more water and then runs away, as if he had just stolen something. Titic stands proudly, his head raised and his ears held straight, but his tongue is hanging out half a meter.

I get up and fetch them a bowl of ordinary water.

We collect our gear and set off home.

Alice is still in the huff at my spoiling her fun.

I buy her some toffees to take her mind off it.

The toffees are as hard as rock.

"Never mind, we'll soak them in some warm water when we get home," I tell her.

Alice is asleep. Ţucu and me are discussing what we should do. In my opinion we should go and have a talk with the school director, but Ţucu is more of a pacifist, he says that we'll get ourselves into a conflict with a madwoman, and anyway, Alice only has another year before she moves up into the fifth form. He says it would be hard to prove any unfairness. Better we talk to her nicely and maybe even bring her a bag of something.

"That's the best way to solve problems," says Ţucu.

"Then you go and talk to her!" I shout at him.

"I will."

When it comes to delicate matters, he's always had more tact.

"Mammy, look, today I got a ten for handwriting!"

"Well done! Now do you see that the comrade has got nothing against you?"

"You were right, Mammy!" she says, rubbing up against me like a cat.

16

Țucu came back from the country on Tuesday afternoon. He was unshaven and sweaty. I made him undress in the hall and I took his clothes straight to the balcony.

"You smell like you brought the cow with you when you came in the house," I said.

He didn't say anything back. He lugged the plastic bags into the kitchen and displayed his trophies on the table. I was happy that he had come back. At least I didn't have to talk to myself anymore. Now I had someone I could joke with. I didn't tell him anything about Alice or our conversation about the elections. I don't think he'd be very interested anyway. Ever since he took up agriculture, he doesn't want to talk about anything else. In the hall it still smells like a barnyard, and so my nostrils start doing some detective work. It wasn't hard to discover that in the grooves of the soles, his shoes had brought back some souvenirs of Catrina's barn. Catrina's yard adjoins the old folks'. You have to live there to know where one garden ends and the next begins. They share a barn too, but only Catrina has a cow now.

"Can you hear?" called Țucu from the kitchen, with his mouth full.

I was in the bathroom, scraping the soles of his shoes with an old razor blade.

"Of course I can hear!"

"What are you doing in there?"

"I'm gouging your shoes . . ."

"I've brought some cheese from the sheepfold . . ."

"From our sheep?"

"What are you talking about? What sheep! We've got a four-legged animal, but the kind that barks, not the kind that produces milk . . ."

"How could you sit on that bus with your shoes in this state?"

"Never mind my shoes. Do you know what I've been thinking? How about we send some to Alin . . ."

"Alain!"

"How about we send him some of this cheese? No Canadian has tasted cheese like this in a million years. We'll give him a surprise."

"Don't forget to send him some butter from Mr. Pardon as well! You're addled in the head! It'll go off by the time it gets to Canada!"

"We'll salt it!"

"I've done a lot of things in my life, but I've never sent cheese by airplane . . ."

"It'll be good for Alice too. Fresh cheese is healthy for pregnant women."

"Alice takes vitamins and whatnot . . ."

"I was just saying . . ."

"Well, don't say!"

"At least come and have a taste. You'll love it . . ."

The kitchen table was full of things: big lovely apples, a bag of cucumbers, a bag of plums, a bag of onions, a dozen eggs, bunches of parsley.

"What did you lay them all out like this for? Don't you know where they go?" I asked, just for the sake of nagging him.

"So you could see them . . ."

"I can see them. Apples, cucumbers, plums . . ."

"So that you'll be convinced that it's worth a lot more than the bus fare."

"There I was thinking that you'd been to the market . . ."

"What a mouth you've got!"

"These cucumbers are big and no mistake."

"Nice, aren't they?"

"Are the eggs from the country too, or did you go to the farm shop?"

"Everything you can see here is from the country."

"What lovely apples! Are these really from your garden?"

"I'm telling you, it's all from the country."

"I thought they must be from the neighbors. Your apples were as big as walnuts . . .."

"That Catrina! Catrina came here, didn't she? I'll wring her neck one of these days, if she can't stop her tongue wagging . . ."

Țucu was bending a piece of wire. He was tallying something up in his head and muttering. I was thinking about Alice.

"What are you doing?" I asked him.

"I'm tiring out this bit of wire."

"You know the elections are on Sunday, don't you?"

"The news has got as far as the country too. Bolohan was giving away free beer on the common. From the back of a truck."

"And?"

"I went and got some . . ."

"Aha. And who are you voting for?"

"Why do I have to vote?"

"Didn't you drink the free beer?"

"The Liberals are giving away pens and I took one of those too . . ."

"Don't let me catch you with it in this house!"

"Don't worry, I lost it . . . The thing is, no matter which way I look at it, I can't vote for the beer and for the pen at the same time . . ."

"I'm talking seriously here, but you . . ."

"I'm not in the mood for talking seriously. Look at this blasted bit of wire!"

"Come on! Who are you going to vote for?"

"Well . . . maybe for the ecologists."

"Who are they?"

"The ones who go on about nature and clean air . . ."

"And what do they promise?"

"Well . . . damn this wire! Well, they'll take cars off the roads, because they cause pollution, and they'll grow vegetables using only natural fertilizer, and it'll be goodbye chemicals . . ."

"How can you vote for them? You're out of your mind!"

"Well, I'll go to the country by horse, clip-clop, good eh? No more cars, no more buses . . . Clean air . . . Exercise and healthiness!"

"Get out of here! All you can do is take the mickey. I was talking seriously."

"Oops, look, I've snapped it. Seriously? Well, to be serious, no matter who gets in, they'll still steal. It doesn't make any difference to me which of them is doing the stealing."

"Is that right? They're all just thieves?"

"Right. If they were honest, they'd stay at home and wouldn't get involved in politics . . . I almost forgot: you haven't even tasted that cheese . . ."

"Yes I have!"

"Well?"

"Is it a bit sour or am I mistaken?"

"You get out of here! It's you who's sour!"

As I was peeling an onion, an idea came to me, which lit up all my little bulbs: instead of sighing and moaning, why don't I do something to bring back the past? Maybe not exactly the way it was, but something similar. A factory was hard to get up and running, but a workshop like the one we had didn't seem impossible to me. My mind started working at full throttle. I started to sweat with excitement. We were old, but we could still work. I even felt in good shape. We could bring in some young people and teach them the trade. The foreman could drum up orders. Oh, yes, it would work for sure. We could make stuff for export. Is there nowhere in the world today where they don't need toolboxes? And what about hinges? Metalwork can't have died off completely. We could work for those ginger Englishmen like in the old days, why not? Or even for the Canadians. The Canadians must use metal products. They're human, after all. There's an idea! Alain could help us. And if it gets off the ground, he could even leave that stupid bank and look after our products. Alice could be a part of it too. We could have a really good workshop, we could laugh and have fun like in the old days. We could have holidays again and have everything our hearts desire. I was becoming more and more enthusiastic about it. I couldn't sit still. The factory didn't necessarily have to be in a factory. It could be in someone's backyard somewhere. Maybe even at Sanda's, now that she's moved back to the country. Sanda wouldn't have any reason to be against it, and she even ought to be proud. Mitu could come too, even if he probably can't work like he used to, but at least he would enliven the atmosphere. Otherwise you work when you feel like it. But I wouldn't invite that idiot Dragoş to come back! Let him die of jealousy! I even thought about how to solve the vehicle problem. We would get some old vehicles that had been written off, and a mechanic would repair them. I know for a fact that a lot of the time they write off perfectly good machinery. I could see with my own eyes how life would start over. We would build a production shed in Sanda's yard. Maybe a small one at first, but we'd expand it after the first export order came in. There was plenty of space there for a warehouse too. Things were coming together and I was more and more delighted with the idea. Aurelia, Ariton, Culidiuc, Sorin and all the others would come home from where they were working abroad. Home to their workshop. Obviously, the foreman would still be the foreman, even if I had come up with the whole idea. Out of respect for what he had done in the past. But also because he knew how to get sheet metal from the Galaţi steelworks and how to drum up orders. Maybe the wages wouldn't be very high in the beginning, I thought, but they would increase later. It would be worth the effort. It would even be worth working for nothing for a while, if need be, because after that the high wages would more than make up for it. We could fill the whole world with toolboxes and brackets, from Russia to Zimbabwe, from Bulgaria to China and even the United States. Only the foreman would be able to make that happen.

Carried away by my idea, I phoned Sanda. It was quite late, but she hadn't gone to bed yet. I decided not to reveal my plan

to her yet, my grand plan for reviving the past, and I just told
her that I wanted to pay her a visit. She asked me whether it was
anything serious and I assured her it wasn't. She probably guessed
something from my voice. I asked her to call Aurelia, if she
could, and we girls would sit and have a gossip. Just like in the
old days. We'd go on Friday afternoon.

17

TUDOR IS ASLEEP in his room. With his bottom lip folded over his top lip he looks funny, like a little man who's disgruntled about something. He's breathing regularly, with his little arms spread out and one little leg resting on the head of a felt monkey. He has more toys than all the children in our village put together. There's a giraffe up on the four-branched light fitting, drinking water from one of the glass lightshades. A plastic crocodile is lying on its back, it's unable to twist back upright, and is going to die of hunger. One of the legs has fallen off a toy tractor—Tudor calls them legs—and has to go to the doctor. A gnome is having a snooze in a pot. Sometimes adult things are more tempting than toys, and so Tudor takes them back to his room. A ladle vanished for a week until it was found under his bed. Another time, he hid two spoons under his mattress. I stand and look at him. He's very dear to me. I'll miss him. A beam of sunlight peeks in through the corner of the window. Pensively, I play with a toy fire engine. How nice it would have been to have dolls! But even without dolls we often used to play together. The house is quiet. I've been living at Uncle Andrei's and Auntie Lucreția's for almost a year. I've learned everything by heart. I've gone out of my way to be useful. They saved me and I'm grateful to them.

I sigh.

I pluck up courage. Let's get on with it, I say to myself.

I get up and leave the boy's room on tiptoes. They are at work. I start to get my things out of the cupboard. I don't have many things and they're not great, but they're the only ones I have. Some of them Auntie Lucreția gave me. Either because

they didn't fit her anymore or because she'd gone off them. These
are the nicest of my things. Should I take them with me? Two
skirts, two dresses, a pair of sandals, a pair of shoes, three blouses
. . . I take them out, carefully fold them, and put them in my
raffia bag. They'll get creased for sure. The lacy blouse, the pullover, the skirt and the broad belt are from Auntie Lucreția. I put
them in the bag, then take them out and put them back in the
cupboard. I take my toothbrush and toothpaste from the bathroom. It was here at their house that I learned to use a toothbrush. I'd never had a large fluffy towel. I find myself going from
room to room. No, I'm not looking for things of mine scattered
around the house, but rather I'm saying farewell. The velvety
sofas, the soft carpets, which I've washed so many times, the
cooker with four rings, the wainscots in the hall . . . I sense that
I'm going to miss all these things. I'm going to miss the racket
Tudor makes and the quiet, peaceful hours in a large and well-
aired house. I'd love to stay! But how can I go on facing Uncle
Andrei every day? How can I look Auntie Lucreția in the eye? In
moments of weakness I'm ready to put all my clothes back in
the cupboard, but I know very well that in a few days, out of
shame, I'll take them out all over again.

No, I can't go and leave Tudor sleeping. I take my bag to the
front door and wait. I'm determined. I can stay for a few weeks
with Corina from school, and then I'll go to a hostel. If not, I'll
find lodgings. Since I've got nothing else to do, I tidy the clothes
on the coatrack. Then I straighten the corner of a curtain and
put the dried dishes in the cupboard. I hear the key turn in the
lock. My heart throbs. I've still got time to change my mind. I've
got one second to do it. No, I have to leave! Who is it? Auntie
Lucreția. I know by the way she opens the door: softly, in case
Tudor is sleeping. Uncle Andrei never thinks of that. I go into
the hall. The front door has knocked my bag over, scattering the
clothes. My face is burning. I tell her before she can say
anything.

"They're mine, Auntie. I'm leaving."

Auntie Lucreția is dressed stylishly. Even since she went to
work in the storeroom, she still looks after herself. Maybe her

nails are a littler shorter, and the varnish gets chipped more often.

"Where are you going? To the cleaner's?"

"No, I'm leaving."

"Yes, but where are you going with all those bags?"

"To Corina's, a girl from school . . ."

"Go on then, have fun . . . When will you be coming back?"

"I'm not coming back . . ."

"Why not? Is anything wrong?"

"No, but I'm not coming back . . ."

"You can't just leave like this, all of a sudden, something must be wrong . . ."

"I don't want to burden you anymore."

"You're not a burden to anyone!"

"I've been intruding too long . . ."

"What are you talking about? Did Andrei say something to you?"

"Oh, no, he didn't! But I just thought that . . ."

"That's enough of your nonsense. Take those bags back inside . . . If you want to go and stay with someone for a couple of days, that's a different story."

I sit down on the corner of the sofa, feeling awkward, cradling the bag of clothes.

Auntie Lucreția comes up to me protectively.

How can I tell her that I saw her kissing another man and that I can't stay in this house anymore?"

18

So, ONE DAY, Ceaușescu, the Great Man, woke up in a foul mood. A really foul mood, and no mistake. He was scowling and muttering to himself. He had a backache and he had had bad dreams. Elena, with her hair looking like a haystack, still wearing her nightdress, was eating sunflower seeds and elegantly spitting the husks into her palm. On the radio, a lady comrade was talking about the role played by the sense of civic duty in the development of socialist democracy in a multilaterally developed socialist society and in Romania's progress to ever new heights of culture and civilization on the luminous path to communism.

"What's with you, Nick? What's wrong with you? What's with that face? It's longer than a Party meeting!" says Elena, the Great Man's comrade in life and work.

"Eh, you know . . ." he said, scratching his crotch.

My apologies to the ladies, but it happens even to Great Men, not just to us nobodies.

"The country's problems?" asks Elena, turning the radio down.

"Nope."

"That awful Gorbachev?"

"Nope."

"That son of yours? I'll go and box his lugs . . ."

"Nope."

"Tell me! Don't keep me on tenterhooks!" says the Great Scientist, spitting sunflower husks onto the carpet in her impatience.

"If you give me some sunflower seeds, I'll tell you!"

"Look at you, you have to pinch mine . . . Can't you get your own?"

"Come on, Lena, don't be stingy!"

"Don't call me Lena!"

"Bunny rabbit!"

"Or bunny rabbit!"

"Gypsy lady . . ."

"You know what, you're an oaf. You've got some nerve!" says Lena. It's her sore spot.

"Come on, Lena, can't you take a joke?" says the Teacup,[1] trying to calm her down.

"Oh, I almost forgot!" says she, clapping her palm to her forehead so loudly that all the glasses in the vitrine rattled. "I was annoyed with you already, because of two days ago."

"What for, comrade wife?"

"Because you tricked me. You keep promising me some crocodile-skin boots, but zilch."

"A good job you reminded me," says the Great Man, remembering. "This afternoon I'll nip over to Egypt and sort it out. No problem."

"On your word?"

"On my word as a pioneer!"

"You, a pioneer?"

"Am too!"

"That's more like it! What kind of seeds do you want? Pumpkin or sunflower? We've got both to choose from, comrade husband. The harvest was good this year, thank God!"

There is a knock on the door and the Great Man quickly pulls on his trousers. Top quality English cloth, not like the overalls us nobodies wear. They'd been nattering away and forgotten all about the time. Lena quickly hides the seeds under the blanket and straightens her hair. She's so beautiful that you'd run a mile. She's a dead ringer for the Wicked Witch of the West.

"Who's there? Is that you, Bobu?" he calls out.

---

1. In Romanian, 'the teacup' is *ceaşca,* which sounds like a shortening of Ceauşescu. – *Translator's note.*

"No, Comrade President. It's me, General Avramescu," comes a voice from behind the door.

"What do you want?"

"We're waiting for you at the long- and short-term strategic council, Comrade Supreme Commander of the Armed Forces."

"Then wait some more, since that's what you get paid for, by the bucket-load!"

"At your orders!"

"That's him told, husband!" says Lena, turning the radio up.

It was the part she liked best, where the listeners phone in. They had to recount their civic deeds. Lena was all ears. Over the radio, a lady comrade recounts:

"I'm a worker and I live in Craiova . . ."

"Hear that, Nick? She's from your neck of the woods. Let's hear what she's got to say."

"A few days ago I was in Bucharest, on personal business. Near the Intercontinental Hotel I found a wallet . . ."

"Yes, and?" asks the comrade radio presenter.

"Obviously, I picked it up and looked inside. I found the sum of five thousand lei and two thousand dollars . . ."

"Lucky her!" exclaims Lena. "I've never found so much as a piece of thread in my whole life."

"The identity papers in the wallet showed that the owner was one Anton Cărăşel and that he lived in Bucharest, on Strada Izvoarelor, at no. 46, building 16, entrance C, flat 3, ground floor . . ."

"What then? What did you decide to do?"

"Well . . . I'd very much like to make a dedication, thanking Comrade Cărăşel . . ."

"Hear that, Nick? You've never phoned in to dedicate a song to me . . ." says Lena sadly.

But Uncle Nick didn't have time to natter, because the generals were waiting for him. And so he told Lena to put some clothes on, so that she wouldn't look like a scarecrow. When he opened the door, General Avramescu was waiting for him. He said that after the meeting the Comrade Supreme Commander had to talk to a Western journalist, that he'd been desperate to talk to him for the past week. But before the Great Man could say anything, his comrade in life and work marched up to the man with epaulettes and said:

"Comrade General, an urgent problem takes us to Egypt. Await further orders."

After the general goes away with his tail between his legs, Lena says sulkily:

"Every tart in the country has crocodile-skin boots except me. What do you say to that?"

What can the Great Man say? They board their plane and rush off to Egypt. On their way, Lena is already chirpier. She takes a handful of seeds out of her handbag and starts munching away. She rips two pages out of Marx's *Capital*, which was on hand for recreational reading, and makes two cornets.

"That's the way to make cornets, comrade. There's an art to it. It's like riding a bicycle: you never forget!"

She puts sunflower seeds in one cornet and pumpkin seeds in the other and offers the Great Man some:

"Help yourself, because they won't last long."

But the Great Man was in no mood to munch seeds. He was pensive. The dream he had that night was troubling him. A stupid dream and all the more disturbing for that. And so he told it to the Great Scientist. He was hunting in the mountains of the Homeland. It was sunny and nice, but no game around. And as he was strolling along in the cool shade of the pine trees, a bearded man appeared, surrounded by a crowd of the unwashed. They stank so badly that even the mosquitos avoided them. And that unwashed rabble tied him up and hauled him off to a cave lit by torches, like he had seen in a film a while ago. There, they started guzzling steaks and quaffing wine, but tossed him nothing but bones. After they had feasted, one of them untied him and shoved him in front of the bearded man, who said to him:

"I am Burebista. Who are you, stranger?"

"I am Ceaușescu. Nicolae Ceaușescu."

The unwashed rabble started to laugh mockingly.

"You, stranger, are the one they call the Genius of the Carpathians?"

"I am he, Burebista!"

The unwashed were splitting their sides, rolling on the ground with laughter.

"Are you sure?"

"I am sure."

"Then if you are the Genius of the Carpathians, I am Little Red Riding Hood!" said the bearded man.

And the unwashed roared with laughter.

The thing that annoyed Ceaşca the most was the bit about Little Red Riding Hood. At least if he'd said: "I don't believe you" or "Let's wrestle like men," he could have understood it, but like that . . .

"I say you're under a spell," said the Great Scientist. "I'll take you to an old woman who'll give you coals quenched in water from a virgin pool and after that you'll sleep like a baby. You'll dream only of roses . . ."

"Can she cure bad backs?"

"Even tonsillitis, if you want . . ."

"But what about you, Lena, just between ourselves . . . You're my wife, after all . . . What do you think? Am I the Genius of the Carpathians?"

"Well . . ."

"Give it to me straight! I'm asking you nicely . . ."

"Well, why not, Nick? What defects do you have? You're no more stupid than other people . . ."

And they both fell asleep, contented.

When they woke up, Lena looked out of the window and cooed:

"Look, Nick! What beautiful rivers our homeland has . . ."

"They're roads, Lena."

"They're rivers!"

"Roads!"

"Rivers!"

"Roads!"

"I say we ask the pilot," says Lena. "Comrade Captain, what are those snaky ribbons down there?"

"Permission to report! They're queues at the food shops, comrade!"

"See, you were wrong!" says Nick, gleefully.

"So were you!"

"Then we're even!"

As soon as they arrived in Egypt, they started looking for crocodile boots. One day passed, then two, then three. Nothing. The generals, with their medals as big as cowbells, were still sitting in the meeting room waiting. Avramescu couldn't take it anymore, so he phones the pilot:

"Comrade Captain, what's going on over there?"

"Comrade General, permission to report! Everything is under control, but I can't say when we will be coming back. Every day, the Comrade and the Lady Comrade go to a river called the Nile—that's N-I-L-E., repeat, Nicolae, Ion, Liviu, Eugen. The Comrade strips to his underpants and goes into the water, and the Lady Comrade sits on the bank in complete safety. The Comrade catches a crocodile, lifts it over his head, and asks: 'Lena, has this one got any boots?' 'No, Nick!' answers the Lady Comrade. This has been going on for three days."

"Very well, comrade Captain! Now do as follows: go to the first leather shop you find, buy a pair of crocodile boots, size 39, and leave them on the riverbank. Don't forget to write a note saying: 'Gift from the Egyptian people.' Understood?"

"Understood, sir!"

On the fourth day, Lena and Nick came back happy. A real bargain! They hadn't been expecting such a reception from the Egyptian people. They were even thinking of making an official visit by way of thanks. But even so, the Great Man was still troubled. He was still disturbed by that stupid dream. And so he summons Avramescu and says:

"Comrade General, this office . . . this office of mine is a bit empty. I'd like to hang a painting over there . . . Find me a good painter, a trustworthy one. Maybe Sabin Bălașa . . . I'd like him

to make me something special . . . I'm thinking of a portrait of
Burebista disguised as Little Red Riding Hood . . ."

And on my horse I rode
To tell the tale I've told.
And if you don't believe it,
You can take it or leave it.

What a wag he is, that Mister Mitu!

19

AT TEN ON the dot, the journalist was at my front door. Cătălin's friend. He looked like a child. I don't think he could have been more than twenty years old. With his long hair in a ponytail, he looked like a girl. Both the knees of his jeans were split and had frayed edges. He wore an earring. "So, this is the type that Cătălin hangs around with," I said to myself. In Ceaușescu's day they used to round them up and chop off their hair, so that they would look like normal people. Nowadays you can't tell which are girls and which are boys anymore.

I invited him into the living room. I'd made some coffee.

"I expect you're here because I'm an old commie . . . Who knows what horror stories that niece of mine has told you . . ."

He laughed. He got out a notebook, a pen and a tape recorder.

"One of these days, they'll stuff me and put me in a museum . . ."

He worked at a weekly paper and wanted to know why people were nostalgic for communism. He asked me to recount my own story.

"Everybody used to call us 'the boyars,'" I said and started to tell him about my life at the workshop, my second job, which I've always missed.

At first it was hard, because I kept looking at the wheels of the cassette turning round and round and it made me feel dizzy. But then I looked elsewhere and I felt better. In the end I forgot about the cassette player and I told him all kinds of memories, sighing the while. I talked a lot about life in our workshop, about

the foreman, about wages, about our team and our good spirits.
I even showed him photographs. One of them, in which I'm
standing with one hand on the compacting machine, the other
on my hip, he took with him to put in the paper. I threatened
him that if he didn't bring it back, I'd go to his boss and kick up
hell until he shaved all his young reporter's hair off. He laughed.
Ţucu poked his head around the door, trying to tempt him with
some cheese and tomatoes, but he declined. He wasn't very talk-
ative. I thought that journalists were supposed to be chatter-
boxes. He asked me what kind of music I listened to back then.
I told him mainly folk music, but we weren't dyed in the wool,
we also listened to Marius Ţeicu, Angela Similea, and Corina
Chiriac. He smiled and then asked me about foreign singers and
groups. I didn't know much about them. All the same, I racked
my brain and came up with two names: Toto Cutugno and Julio
Iglesias, although to be honest I was never all that keen on them.
Ah, he also asked me who Bobu and Postelnicu were. I was surprised he didn't know.

As he was leaving, I couldn't help myself and I asked him how
old he was.

"I was ten when the Revolution came!"

He was too young to remember the school textbooks with
the photograph of Ceauşescu on the first page—that photograph
in which you can see just one of his ears.

That afternoon, I don't know what got into me, but I decided
to pay Mrs. Rozalia a visit. I phoned her and she told me she
could receive me. She's strange, Mrs. Rozalia. You can't just turn
up at her house and ring the bell, like you would with any other
neighbor. No, you always have to phone in advance. If you've
run out of pepper and think she might be able to lend you some,
first you have to talk to her on the phone. Even though we've
lived on the same landing for twenty years, we still address each
other with the formal "you." She's like that with everybody, not
just me. She's a seamstress by trade and back in the day, when
money wasn't a problem, I often used to take my sewing to her.
Now she's elderly and it takes her five attempts before she can

thread a needle. She only does small jobs now, like taking up a hem. I think she is seven or eight years older than me. For a time she was a part-time drawing teacher in a village nearby. She gave up because of the commute. Although her husband was an agronomist, since he worked mainly in an office they used to have problems obtaining food. That's why we used to bring her this and that. I often wondered why she couldn't manage when it came to food, given she wasn't just a skilled seamstress, but also an imaginative one: you wouldn't believe the caliber of clients she had. She must have had money, so why couldn't she manage? From the wives of Party first secretaries to lady doctors and sales assistants at the department store, women from every walk of life went to her, but she didn't have so much as a packet of butter in her fridge. Țucu said it was out of delicacy. She was too embarrassed to bring up the matter of food. That might have been it. The truth is that she always had an air about her . . . I don't know how to put it . . . an air of being very special. When I brought her two salamis and a packet of ground coffee, instead of being delighted, she would look at me in embarrassment. I knew she needed them; it was obvious. And she would pay me or else do some sewing for me in exchange, since I didn't give her them like she was a beggar. I caught on that she felt uncomfortable, and so I didn't hand them to her, but left them by the sofa in a bag. The very first time I laid eyes on her, I said to myself that Mrs. Rozalia is a different kind of town-dweller than Auntie Lucreția. She had a different kind of smile, a gentler one. She walked as softly as a cat; you never heard her heels clacking. She wore her hair in a small bun. I looked at her nails, of course. She used a pale varnish. Never red. I liked her, although we never talked about anything except colors, stitches and seams. In fact no, I tell a lie, we did use to talk about Alice. She was always interested in how the little girl was doing. When she got into university, she congratulated me, with a very warm smile. When I wanted her to make something for me, it used to take ages to choose the pattern. She wasn't like other seamstresses who make whatever you want. No, you had to discuss it with her, leaf through German and French magazines, tell her exactly what kind of occasion you wanted it for, go over all the details. I often used to go away having ordered something different than I had had in mind. But she didn't force you. She would smile gently and talk to you almost in a whisper, as if somebody were asleep in the next room. And I can say I was never disappointed.

The flat hadn't changed much. I hadn't been inside her flat for years, but it was still just as clean and simple. She hadn't taken down the two paintings in the hall, which, from what I was once told, she had painted in her youth. In passing, I cast a glance inside the room she used as a workshop. The lid was on the sewing machine and there were no longer pieces of material strewn everywhere. Now, the room looked just like any other. Back then, it used to be strange, the difference between the mess in the workshop and the tidiness in the rest of the house. In the living room I saw the same brass candlesticks and the same old wooden clock. Not a trace of any ornaments. The other girls from work and I were proud of our knickknacks, which were somehow a sign of wealth, but you never found any in Mrs. Rozalia's house. Not that she couldn't afford them. I once gave her a Chinese figurine, an old man leaning on a staff, but I never saw her put it on display. I didn't get upset. I knew that you could never be sure how Mrs. Rozalia would react. I always found her unpredictable.

On the little table between the armchairs there was a tray with two saucers of jam and two glasses of cold water. The same tray, the same saucers, the same teaspoons as in the old days, as if time had stood still. Mrs. Rozalia was wearing a pullover and trousers, with her hair tied up in a tight bun. She was smiling calmly. On the phone she had warned me that she didn't work anymore, and so she was probably waiting to see what the purpose of my visit could be. But not even I was very sure what it was. As a result, the conversation ground to a halt. Somehow, I would have liked to know what she thought about communism, how she saw things. Maybe if Auntie Lucreția had still been alive, I would have felt the need to talk to her, but as it was, Mrs. Rozalia was the one who resembled her the most. Although at the same time they were very different. Auntie Lucreția died a few years before the Revolution. Maybe the reason I was there was also because Mrs. Rozalia cared so much about Alice, in her own, distant way. And so I started telling her about Alice. Hearing the news that "the little girl" was going to have a baby, Mrs. Rozalia flushed.

"Lord, how time flies . . ." she murmured.

The atmosphere relaxed. It was very pleasant, the way she patiently listened and answered in a whisper. Finally, I confessed to her about the discussion I had had with Alice, about the misunderstanding between us. Mrs. Rozalia was all eyes and ears. She gave a rather awkward smile and told me more directly than I had been expecting:

"My dear, I'm sorry, but I think the girl is right."

Then I asked her just as directly:

"Mrs. Rozalia, if you don't mind my asking, who will you be voting for?"

"I don't mind your asking at all! I'll be voting for the Liberals."

I gave a start. My shock was more obvious than I would have liked. She had caught me completely off guard. For me, the Liberals were the worst of the worst. They wanted to take all the factories away from the state and give them to the private sector—to steal them, in other words. They were even flirting with the idea of selling them for a dollar to foreigners, who would then supposedly invest in them and make them profitable. I could almost picture the foreigners' commission money flowing into the Liberals' pockets.

"But why?" I blurted.

Mrs. Rozalia smiled reassuringly.

"I know . . . anyway . . . you have different opinions . . . But if you have the patience to listen, I would like to tell you something."

20

IT'S FRIDAY EVENING and I'm waiting for Sanda at the bus station. Last week, via somebody from the village, she sent word to me that she would be coming to see me. She probably had to pester our parents until they let her. Who knows what she must have promised them in exchange! Buses are few and far between and the bus station is swarming. All the benches are taken and so I'm walking up and down. Folk are sitting with their bags clenched between their knees, as if thieves could strike at any moment. I gawp at the bus timetable and I'm amazed at all the places that can exist. I think there must be hundreds of villages in this world apart from ours. But it doesn't hit you until you see a list of them. You can live in a village all your life without knowing anything except what's around you. Idle thoughts! The bus arrives in a cloud of dust. It's a jalopy that rattles from every joint and reeks of diesel. I know it well. I get a harebrained idea. I hide around a corner and watch as the passengers alight, sweating, lugging their bags. Sanda's head appears in the door of the bus. She's wearing a white headscarf with blue dots. Isn't she hot? She stands in front of the bus, holding a plastic bag, without budging. Put it down, I tell her in my mind. The folk slowly disperse. A guy from my village passes and says:

"Look, your sister's over there!"

"I know," I answer, giggling.

Sanda asks an elderly man what time it is. He lifts his head and gazes around. Wiping his hands with a rag, the driver says something to her and laughs, but she doesn't look very amused. She shifts the bag from one hand to another, but she doesn't put

it down. She is flushed. She asks what time it is again. She keeps
craning her neck. The bus reverses a little way, turns around, and
envelops Sanda in a whirl of black smoke. She moves two steps
away, but not too far, as if she's frightened she might get lost. If
I remember rightly, she's only been to town twice before: once
to the hospital, in an ambulance, and once to Uncle Andrei's and
Auntie Lucreţia's, with Father. She looks like a frightened hen. I
show myself, before she starts wailing. She sees me. I can see the
joy in her eyes.

"Lord, what a fright I got! I thought that Sandu mustn't have
passed on the message . . . or that you'd forgotten . . ."

We hug each other.

"He came to see me and I told him to tell you that I'd be
waiting for you round the corner . . ."

I start to laugh.

"You liar!" she says, about to get annoyed.

"You'll see what it's like in town . . . That was your
initiation."

We go to the hostel, in the industrial district. Sanda is still in
the huff. She didn't appreciate my joke. She says I'm putting
on town airs. The hostel isn't far from the factory where I work.
I've been there for a year. It's the first time I've had money of
my own and I'm very proud. I've even bought myself a few
clothes. My other ones had started looking too old. There's
construction work going on everywhere and so the journey is
a bit arduous. We have to cross ditches, step over pipes, avoid
cables. They're building eight-storey tenement blocks for the
workers. When it rains it's like a disaster zone. The only way
to avoid the mud is by taking the town ring road. I live in a
room with three other girls. Adriana is going to her parents'
tomorrow, and so Sanda can sleep in her bed. But tonight we'll
both have to squeeze into the same bed. It's not quite like at
Auntie Lucreţia's, but it's all right.

"We've got two days to do whatever we like," I tell her. "Think
about what you fancy doing . . ."

"I'd like to go and see the train."

"You'll be able to hear it from my room . . . But we'll go and you can see it up close."

At the hostel, Adriana is doing Livia's hair. Since she knows a bit about hairdressing, every now and then she sits us on a stool, wraps a sheet around our neck and gives us a trim. It's so that she can keep her hand in and so that we don't have an extra expense. Maria is showing them photographs of actors. Apparently you can buy them from the newspaper stand. I personally wouldn't spend my money on that kind of thing.

"Look at his hairstyle!" cries Maria.

Livia looks with an expert eye, from different angles.

"Hmm, yes, I could do a cut like that . . ."

"Let me see," says Adriana, taking the photograph. "Never mind his haircut, look at how handsome he is! I think I'll see him in my dreams tonight!"

"What do you expect, if he's an actor!" comments Maria.

"I'll dream of him in whatever film I like," laughs Adriana.

The girls talk about actors and the films they've been in.

We each take a turn looking at the photograph. I don't recognize any of them. Nor does Sanda. But they're handsome, it's true, and they're dressed really smartly. Our village wasn't electrified until a few years ago. I've only been to the cinema here twice. After we eat, I ask Sanda whether she'd like to watch television. She's delighted. I take her to the recreation room on the ground floor, where we have to attend plenary Party meetings when they're held. There are a few other girls here. I write the number of my room on Sanda's hand so that she won't forget and then I go back upstairs. I iron a few clothes.

Sanda comes back later, disappointed.

"Are you sure the guys in those photos are actors? I watched for ages and I didn't see any of them."

"You can watch tomorrow and maybe you'll have more luck."

In the morning I ask her which she'd prefer: to go to a cake shop, to look at the shop windows, to have a walk in the park, or to go to the cinema. But before anything else Sanda wants to go and see the train. Picking our way through the potholes, we go to the station. The shunting yard is nearer the hostel than the station itself. On the way, we buy some warm bagels from the booth in front of the bread factory. Sanda loves bagels. She'd like to take a few back with her to the country, but I warn her that as soon as they stop being fresh, they become as tough as the sole of a boot.

"Have you ever gone anywhere by train?" she asks.

"Of course!"

I'd visited the parents of one of the girls from work, in the country. I was amazed that their village had a station. But in fact it didn't. We went twenty kilometers by train and got off at a stop that wasn't even a proper station, and then we had to walk another seven kilometers across the fields. But I could still say I'd been on a train, couldn't I?

"What was it like?" asks Sanda.

"It was nice . . ."

We reach the railway and walk along the tracks. Near some silos we spot a bogie on a siding. I explain to her that the railway cars run along the metal rails. She stoops to touch them:

"How cold they are!"

"Because they're iron."

We come up to some railway carriages. They are dripping water. I explain to Sanda that they've probably just been washed. She takes two steps back and counts the carriages. Fourteen. We hear a whistle. A goods train is passing a few tracks away. My sister watches it until it vanishes.

"What a loud noise it makes!" she shouts, tugging at her earlobes.

"The sound of iron on iron, that's why!"

"Look, this one's door is open!" she calls out in surprise.

"It's not like a flat where you need to lock it . . . Do you want to climb up?"

She nods. The steps have been raised and so I give her a leg up. Once she's inside, she reaches down to pull me up. We walk a few paces down the corridor. Sanda waves from one of the windows and cries:

"Bye-e-e-e! I'm off to Bucharest . . ."

"Maybe somebody will see us and ask for our tickets," I say.

Sanda quickly pulls her head back inside. A few drops of water have landed on the back of her neck. We go inside one of the compartments. Sanda plonks herself down on one of the banquettes, as if testing the springs on a new bed. She runs her finger over the vinyl cover. She reads the announcements. She looks at the photographs under the pane of glass fastened with nickel-coated screws: a mountain landscape and lots of sea views.

"Does this train only go to the mountains and the seaside?" she asks.

"I've no idea . . . I think that's where it must go most often . . ."

"What's this, an alarm signal?"

"That's right, if someone feels ill, you can sound the alarm."

"Then what happens?"

"Well, I think a doctor comes . . . someone to give you first aid . . ."

Sanda is satisfied with my explanations and so we walk to the end of the carriage. We discover that you can go from one carriage to the next.

"Look, it even has a toilet!" I say, in amazement.

"But you said you'd been on a train before!"

"I have been on one, but I didn't need to go to the toilet."

Sanda is as delighted as a small child. She's hopping around. The carriage we've just entered is a lot cleaner, and instead of benches, there are seats with plush upholstery. Not even I have seen anything like it. We each sink into a chair, enjoying the softness. Sanda closes her eyes in pleasure. It's just like at Auntie Lucreția's, I think to myself.

"I reckon these seats are for Party members," says Sanda.

"That's what I reckon, too."

A jolt awakens us from our reverie. The carriage has started moving. We leap to our feet in fright. We dash to the nearest door. We jump out, without using the steps, like when we were little and just to jump down from a tree. We both calm down and start to laugh.

"We almost ended up in Bucharest," she says.

The train comes to a stop.

21

It's nine in the morning and we're working like crazy. We're giving it our all, so that we can take it easy after the break. The doorbell, loud and hoarse, like a hooter, announces there's someone at the door, a stranger. The bolt is drawn and the foreman appears, with a face like a funeral. Next to him, an elegant man holding a cigarette, none too jolly either. Aurelia whispers to me that it's the new director. I heard a few months ago that they'd changed the director, but I hadn't had a chance to see his mug until now. Shaven to the bone, with an impeccable haircut, but forbidding at first sight. I'm thinking that the foreman is in hot water or that one of us has put our foot in it, really deep, if the director has condescended to take his fancy suit for a walk among our greasy overalls. Comrade Suit puts his hands over his ears and scrunches up his eyes, and the foreman makes a sign for us to shut down the machinery. As soon as you can hear yourself think, the foreman tells us to gather around, because the comrade director general has an announcement for us. We form a circle around him. Comrade Suit stubs out his cigarette end with the toe of his 420-lei-a-pair shoe, clasps his hands together, and lets rip, solemnly:

"Dear comrades, I have some good news for us all. Because your workshop has for many years been foremost in 'Socialist Competition,' the comrades from the County branch of the Party have entrusted us with a lofty and privileged mission."

We're obviously in for it now, I tell myself. They're probably going to increase our hours.

"A mission of which we should be proud. That of presenting

and making known the fruits of our labor at the highest level possible, to Comrade Nicolae Ceauşescu . . ."

Blah, blah, blah. We all freeze to the spot. In three days, Ceauşescu is going to visit our workshop, to stimulate production for export.

"Please start preparing for this edifying moment immediately!" the director concludes his speech.

This means military discipline; we all know it.

Old man Mitu has a pasteurized look about him, as he himself puts it. Either he's got a hangover, or his morning dose of holy water was a bit too large.

The foreman tries to obtain a day's delay from the director, before commencing the cleanup, because we have to finish an order for Thailand. Any delay will result in docked wages.

"Comrade, Ceauşescu is coming, don't you understand? Is export what matters to us now?" the director snaps at him, lighting another cigarette.

They both go out, and we remain, pensive.

"On my life, I won't budge until I take a photo of Ceauşescu right here next to my lathe," says Mister Mitu, chewing his words.

"Old man Mitu, if Ceauşescu shakes hands with you, you won't wash until your dying day," Pancu goads him.

"No-o-o-o, I want a kiss from Lena. I'm going to dress up as a pioneer and give her flowers, just so she'll give me a peck on the cheek."

We all laugh, but without pleasure.

The foreman comes back sharpish. He reads Mister Mitu at a glance and sends him off to sleep for an hour. He hasn't managed to budge the director when it comes to a delay, so we all get ready to make the whole place squeaky-clean. He warns us that if we don't make a good job of it, we'll all be in the lurch. The director, especially given that he's new, is also quaking in his underpants, so he'll be keeping a close eye on us in the days to come. In three days and three nights we'll have to sort out everything that hasn't been repaired or cleaned for the last twenty years. If need be, we'll work in shifts. We won't be alone, because the entire factory will be in on the act. Our workshop has been picked out, but you never know where Ceauşescu will have a mind to poke his nose in. I've never seen the foreman so agitated. He's talking and walking among us. He's thinking out loud. He's giving orders for today and the following days.

He changes his mind. He contradicts himself. He stutters.

He's in a panic!

In the end, we manage to get our act together somewhat. We decide to start with the whitewashing, because that makes the most mess. Then we'll go on to painting everything that hasn't seen a paintbrush for years, cleaning the windows, polishing the machinery, and after that we'll see.

The scurrying begins. At first we all get under each other's feet, but little by little we each settle down to business. Where they've passed by with the whitewash, Aurelia and me clean up the splashes and do the windows. Sanda couldn't be luckier—she's on maternity leave.

It's afternoon already and things are progressing nicely, but we're far from having finished. We've only had a quarter of an hour break. My back is aching and my hands are stinging. At first, Aurelia and me chatted about this and that, but now we're working in silence. The only thing you can hear is the swishing of the brush and the creaking of the windows.

From the storeroom appear two women with piles of overalls and all kinds of protective gear. We're given new kit. On the day of the visit we'll have to look like in the textbook, as the foreman says. With helmets and goggles, with gloves and leather aprons where necessary.

On this occasion, the foreman decrees a break. He sends someone out to buy food for all the others. Plus mineral water, in spite of some murmured protests. He fetches coffee from his own office.

Each person has to sign for the new kit. For the first time ever, the people from stores have the patience to let us try the gear on first. Before, they always used to give it to us and that would be that. If the overalls were too small or too large, you would have to pester them for a week before they would change them for you. We lay out the table for everyone, and we go off one at a time and come back with our kit under our arm. We munch without speaking, each lost in his own thoughts.

Old man Mitu appears, with a helmet on his head, goggles, apron and bulky pigskin gloves. He walks swaying, with his arms spread out in front of him, as though he wanted to throttle somebody.

"My name is Dumitru Prunariu," he says, "the first Romanian in space. On this solemn occasion, I wish to bring you greetings from our Martian friends."

I take advantage of the moment of relaxation to make a phone call to Ţucu and tell him I don't know when I'll be getting back. He's just got back, seconds after Alice, and is warming up the dinner. I explain to him what it's all about and he says he knows about Ceauşescu's visit, that they've been mobilized too, and that he'll tell me all about it at home. Today they got away quickly, but tomorrow looks set to be grim. I ask him to take Alice around to Sanda's, for a day or two, until the storm blows over. It's not the first time the girl will have stayed at her auntie's, because they get on really well.

The street is all a bustle too. Barrels of tar are boiling, and the dump trucks are unloading asphalt. Down the hill, the steam-rollers are already at work. At last, they are laying some asphalt round here. Up to now, you had to do the slalom in the car just to avoid the potholes. By the entrance, up the hill, the tall dusty pines are being hosed down. Next to our fence, facing the street, mounds of black earth are being carried off in buckets. The gravel and dry grass disappear, and here and there flowerbeds are being made. The watchmen are painting the large gate at the vehicles entrance.

The other sections aren't sitting idle either. Everyone is on the move. Inside, they've already got to the painting stage. First of all, we do the flange that runs around the workshop, then we do the metal parts, the posts and all the rest. Everything in green. Although the windows are wide open, the paint fumes are making us dizzy.

It's ten o'clock at night and, the same as everywhere else in town, the power has been cut off.

We light a few lanterns, but you can't see much. The foreman is in despair. He's talking on the phone in his office. He's roaring:

"Ceauşescu is coming, don't you understand? Turn the power on, otherwise it will be you who has to answer for it."

We wait. We're exhausted. The foreman keeps making phone calls. Not even Mister Mitu has any more appetite for jokes.

At last, the electricity comes back on and, grudgingly, we start work again. We don't make much headway. He leaves us to it for another hour and then lets us go home. When I get back, Ţucu is asleep. I don't wake him. I fall asleep like a log.

Here we are the next day, at the crack of dawn. Among us, two unknown persons in new overalls. The foreman makes the introductions, glumly:

"These are your new colleagues. They are called Andrei and Maria. They will be the workers' representatives in the official delegation that will accompany the Comrade President. Now they will give us a helping hand and familiarize themselves with the workplace."

Andrei is athletic, with short hair. Judging from his jaw, I would sooner see him in shorts and boxing gloves than in overalls. Maria is very pretty, just right for handing over flowers.

The plan for today is as follows: in the morning we'll finish painting inside and polish all the machinery until you can see your face in it, and in the afternoon we'll move on to fixing up the exterior. I'm in the same crew as Aurelia again. We start on the machinery. We scour the oil-soaked dust from all the crannies, scrub with emery paper, and buff with felt. The foreman passes the word on, from one to another, that we should mind what we say in front of the new pair. There wasn't any need to tell us. The hardest will be for old man Mitu, who has a bit of a loose tongue.

I peek from the corner of my eye at our new workmates. Andrei is looking at a lathe like it were a giraffe, and it's as though Maria were holding a hedgehog not a rag.

"It's hard to change your trade from one day to the next," I whisper to Aurelia.

Aurelia chuckles to herself.

Comrade Suit passes by to see how the work is going and to encourage us.

At one point, Maria comes over to us. She asks us for a plaster, because she has got a blister from the emery paper. She has delicate hands, but the nails are not polished. I bring her a roll of leucoplast from the first aid kit, to cut off as much as she wants. She asks us if we usually work like this.

"Not quite at this pace, but it's hard work," says Aurelia prudently.

Maria stays next to us. She has begun to get used to it and is scrubbing vigorously. She tells us she has a kid in the fourth form and that the lessons are hard, they have a whole heap of subjects. I say that it's better that way, so that they'll get used to hard work from an early age. After that I regret saying it. Who knows how she'll interpret it.

We continue scrubbing in silence.

The foreman calls me to one side and tells me it's my turn to go and talk to the secret policeman responsible for the factory. He explains which office I have to go to. He tells me not to be frightened. It's nothing serious. Everyone has to go.

22

'THE BOYARS' IS what they all used to call us. Our workshop produced goods for export and it was we who brought the hard currency in. Back then, Ceaușescu wanted to pay off the foreign debt, so that the West would stop weighing us down with interest payments, and that's why hard currency was precious. All the good stuff was exported. If goods were rejected, for example a shipment of shoes made for the West, folk would be fighting each other for them when they reached the shops here. There'd be huge lines. We made all kinds of metal products, and so if they were rejected, they were scrapped and there would be a huge scandal. A commotion. Docked wages. We had to be very careful, but the pay was good. We got more than double what other people got. On payday, when the accountant arrived with the money, we would lock the doors of the workshop so that the other workers in the factory wouldn't find out how much we got. Mum's the word, the foreman used to tell us. But we worked hard for it, we'd cry: we didn't steal it! We said that, but we knew the foreman was right.

In our workshop it was like we were on a different planet. At the back, in a kind of storeroom, we had a bathtub, where the cold water was always flowing. That's where we kept the beer and the juice. When you felt like it, you'd quaff a beer. Obviously, alcohol was banned in the factory. Right above the bathtub, as a joke, we'd even stuck up a plaque stating Article 400, which punished consumption of alcohol in the workplace. The gatekeepers used to search us to check we weren't smuggling any bottles inside. "Where's the fuel?" they'd ask. They searched the

men very thoroughly. They searched everywhere except under
the fillings in their teeth. Even though they never found anything on anybody, the workers all had red noses when they finished their shifts. The truth is they drank like there was no
tomorrow. But they also worked hard! In our workshop, Mister
Mitu didn't even sit down at his machine until he'd fetched himself a bottle of the hard stuff. He didn't have any truck with
drinks for the ladies, as he liked to call them. He wouldn't even
use beer as mouthwash, as he used to say, with a laugh. But when
Mister Mitu sat down at his machine, he used to roll off the parts
like a conveyor belt. He was like a robot. It was the foreman who
brought us beer, by the crate. Who would have dared search his
car? He was the one who earned the hard currency. It was thanks
to him that we always came top of the socialist production league
table. The gatekeepers used to greet him like he was the director
himself. They were paid in rotation, by a different section every
month. When they got paid by our section, they couldn't believe
how much money they received. "Take a photograph," the foreman told them, "because it'll be a while before you see money
like that again." The ones that were on our side, the ones who
told us if there was going to be an inspection or whatever, and
who didn't cause us any trouble, used to get paid by our section
the most often. The ones that didn't could wait until their hair
started growing through their caps. The blokes from the other
sections didn't know how we managed it when it came to drinks,
not that they themselves ever died of thirst. I used to see some
of them climbing over the fence next to our workshop, which
was around the corner and more out of the way. Then, they'd
nip off to the shop. I used to hear that others used to sneak booze
into the factory hidden in jars. They'd buy a jar of cherry com-
pote, let's say, pour out the juice and then top it up with liquor.
They'd leave the fruit inside. Then, they'd seal the lid and the
gatekeepers could search their bags a hundred times without
finding the booze. Romanians are nothing if not inventive!

It was a good life!

Well, we'd finish our work for the day before the lunch break.
It would be around eleven, half past eleven. We started work at

six o'clock in the morning. After the break we'd be free to do what we wanted. We'd keep the machinery running so that from outside they could hear the rumble and think we were working, and we'd each get on with our own business. If you wanted to go to do some shopping, there was nothing to stop you. But after taking a shower, most of us would play different kinds of games. I can see Ariton and Sorin in my mind's eye. They were always playing backgammon. They were mad for it. Sometimes they'd hold championships with a number of players. There would be laughter and teasing. Costel, Radu, Pancu and Aldea played cards. Each with a beer by his leg, like soldiers with their rifles. Others played dice. It was like at a casino, on my word. If there was a Party inspection, the gatekeepers would immediately send us word and we'd all be at our machines, working industriously. In any case, we always kept the door locked. Whoever wanted to enter had to ring the doorbell. If it was one of our lot, he'd give two long rings followed by a short one, so that we wouldn't have to go through the whole charade of pretending to be at work. Culidiuc was the quietest. He'd find a corner and have a nap. He had a house with a small garden. And so when he got off work he had to be rested, ready to work in his garden. If you felt like it, you could make things for people, to earn money on the side. The foreman didn't look very kindly on that sort of thing. He said we earned enough not to have to work on the side. If the police caught one of us with the parts to make window frames to close in a balcony, we'd all be in the lurch, and so he kept his eyes on us. But he didn't intervene if it was something for a relative. There was one guy, Plugaru, who was always at the hole-punch machine, always welding something . . .

"What are you up to there, Plugaru?" the foreman would ask.

"I'm just making a plant pot stand for a nephew, foreman."

"Just how many nephews have you got? You've been making them stands for ten years already."

"Lots of them, they're from the country, and I had ten brothers."

"And now all of them have moved to the town?"

"All of them, boss, not one is left in the country."

"But they all like to grow flowers, I see!"

In the sections where wages were low, they all did work on the side. The hen pecks up her food where she scratches the ground. That's what they used to say. They made enough window frames to close in balconies for an entire district of tower blocks. They made enough tomb grilles for all the people who died in the Second World War. True, they had the materials back then. Nowadays, you'd have to search long and hard to find a scrap of pipe in a Romanian factory. Everything has gone down the drain.

There were just three of us girls: me, my sister Sanda, and Aurelia. We didn't join in the games very much. Cards every now and then. We would knit or go and do our shopping. Sometimes we would make metal boxes, for needles and buttons. We'd give them away as presents or sell them for ten lei each. Sometimes we even made big toolboxes. They sold for twenty-five lei. Anyway, we had enough to live on, because our wage packets were big, and that's no joke. We had so much fun at work that at the end of the day we'd be sorry to go home.

And the parties we had! When it was a special occasion, we'd have a real feast. In the storeroom at the back. We'd have everything: salami, cheese, tomatoes, pasties, and, sometimes, even olives. They were quite hard to find. There'd be beer, juice, everything. We even listened to music, because the machinery drowned it out so nobody else could hear. It was nice. That's when Mister Mitu would tell us his jokes. But he didn't tell just one joke at a time, like most people do. Mister Mitu used to string them together like a bead necklace. No sooner had he told one than he'd go on to another, and then another. Your belly ached from laughing so hard, on my word! When he was on a roll, it was lethal. Mister Mitu also told all those stories about Nick and Lena. The way he told them! You'd think you were there in the bedroom with them. I could picture them bickering with each other, like husband and wife. Obviously, it was all made up, but it was so over the top that you couldn't help but burst out laughing. He'd keep his bottle close by, so he wouldn't have to stretch out his hand when he got thirsty, and he'd begin:

"So, one day, Ceauşescu, the Great Man, woke up in a foul mood. A really foul mood and no mistake."

When we heard him begin, we'd all fall silent and listen with baited breath. Mister Mitu came to work in our section late on. He'd worked in the screws section before that. He must have had really good connections to have got such a cushy job in our section. And he'd take another swig from his bottle and tell some more tall tales.

Oh, how we used to laugh!

True, sometimes we laughed out of fear.

They'd tell him:

"Mister Mitu, you'll get us all thrown into jail with those stories of yours."

"Leave it out, the boss isn't looking," he'd say, unconcerned.

We never got into trouble because of the jokes, but we almost came a cropper because of something else. Once, we got an order from England, for some metal boxes with all kinds of holes in them. I don't know what the gingers were going to use them for. We were over the moon, as you can imagine. It meant hard currency. And big wage packets, obviously. There were some who made fun of us, saying that the English just wanted them for the metal, not for the boxes. In other words, all they were interested in was the iron, because Ceauşescu didn't sell raw materials. They were going to melt them down and make them into razor blades, they said. A young guy had just joined our section, Dragoş. In fact, we'd had to take him because he was the nephew of the Party first secretary. The foreman didn't have any choice. Since he didn't know one end of a pair of pliers from the other, the foreman assigned him design work, because there was never anything to do in that department, except once in a blue moon. The boxes for the English weren't anything complicated, and so the foreman set him to work designing them. We got down to work. We toiled away like we were possessed and the first shipment of three thousand boxes was ready in a week. When quality control came to check them, they almost fainted. The two holes on the left should have been on the right. Not three hundred, but three thousand boxes. If it hadn't been the first secretary's nephew who was to blame, it would have been a real disaster. And so they hushed it up. It was the foreman who sorted it out in the end. He took the boxes to the scrap heap and they compacted them on the spot. They made the sign of the cross when they saw what good quality material it was. Then through a connection he got some sheet metal from the steelworks in Galați and we set to work again. Obviously, each of us kept as many boxes as we could carry. We sold them left and right and still had a few left over. I think that even today, if you go to the flea market, you can still find those boxes for the English.

But today you have to search long and hard for a shred of sheet metal in a Romanian factory. Everything has gone down the drain.

23

SANDA LOVES IT in the town. We go for a walk in the park and look at the statues. We know who the writers are, but we haven't heard of the others.

"It's like these benches and statues were in a forest," murmurs Sanda.

We soon get bored and head to the cake shop. I know what I want: a bar of Africana chocolate and a juice, but my sister takes a long time deciding what she wants. She reads each label and asks me what each thing tastes like. I haven't tasted them all, and so I can't tell her what some of the things are like. She's narrowed it down to three different cakes, but she can't decide between them.

"Have one of each, if you've got an appetite," I urge her.

That's just what she does and we fill our table. The woman behind the counter smiles. By the time I finish my Africana, she's guzzled the lot. She scrapes each plate in turn with her spoon.

"Want some more?" I ask.

"No, they're a bit too sweet . . ."

It's not until we move on to our juice that we start to talk. She tells me the news from home and I tell her about my new life. She thinks it doesn't even compare with what I left behind and that it was a good thing I ran away. She sighs.

"You know, Mica . . . I also came because I wanted to ask you something . . ."

"Let's hear it!"

"Well, I wanted to ask you . . . I don't know, but do you think you could find a trades school for me too?"

I don't say anything. I look at my plate.

"What do you say?" she insists.

"Mother and Father will kill me."

"Maybe not . . . What do you say?"

"I'll try."

"Promise?"

"Do I have any choice?"

We change the subject. I talk about my old teachers from school and we laugh at them. We describe each of them, exaggerating their defects. We're having lots of fun. But when I find out that our math teacher, Sebastian Protopopescu, has left the village, I feel sad. I don't know why exactly. I pay and we leave. Sanda asks how much it cost, but I tell her it's none of her business. On the way, we buy ice cream cones. We look in the shop windows. There are still things to see in the shop windows, because the hard times won't come until a few years later. We go to the new department store. It has two floors and lots of departments. One of the assistants tells us we can't come in with our ice creams, and so we wolf them down. We look at the shoes, the textiles, the sports ware, the cosmetics, the porcelain, and the men's and women's clothing. I ask her to choose something, so I can buy her it as a present. When she hears that, we have to look at everything all over again. I spot a green hat that Father might like, for special occasions, and I ask to see it. Sanda tries it on, because I think my head's a bit too big. I buy it. Sanda tries on a pair of sunglasses. They suit her.

"They're just perfect for when you're treading manure!" I laugh.

I pay for them and we look at the rest of the shop. Sanda stops in front of every mirror to admire herself. She's thrilled with the sunglasses. She keeps adjusting them on her nose, moving them back and forward. We agree that the best thing to buy Mother would be a headscarf. We look everywhere, but can't find any. I suggest that maybe we'll have better luck elsewhere. As we are leaving the department store, I spot a familiar outline. It's Auntie Lucreția. She is standing in the entrance with her back to us. She looks like she is waiting for somebody. I grab Sanda's arm and signal her not to say anything. I'm scared to see whom Auntie Lucreția might be meeting.

"Let's go and walk some more," I whisper to Sanda. "She'll get annoyed that we didn't stop by and visit her."

But my sister doesn't seem very taken with my suggestion. She stands still, unable to come to a decision.

"Look who we have here!" we hear somebody say behind us. It's Uncle Andrei.

All four of us stand together talking in front of the shop, getting in the way of the people coming in and out. We find out that they are going to a wedding party tonight and have been looking for a present. I breathe a sigh of relief. We don't have to visit them. Some other time. Auntie Lucreția looks very elegant, as usual. We part. The two of us set out in search of a headscarf, and on the way we buy another two ice cream cones. I tell Sanda not to lick her fingers. I give her my handkerchief. We stop to look in the window of a sports ware shop. We go in and Sanda tries on a pair of Chinese tennis shoes. You can see from her face that she doesn't even want to take them off, and so I pay for them. Sanda gives me a kiss.

We chatter as we walk along.

"What's that?"

"The steam baths."

"What do you mean? You wash with steam? Doesn't it scald you?"

"You wash with soap and water, but you sit in the steam . . ."

"Doesn't it suffocate you?"

"You get used to it . . ."

"I'd rather use suds . . ."

In the evening, Sanda goes to watch the actors again. Maybe she'll have more luck this time.

It's afternoon and we're at the bus station. I'm seeing Sanda off. She's sulking because she has to go back. There weren't any tickets for the evening bus and so she has to travel in the afternoon heat. She has a big heavy bag. Besides the presents, she has loaves of bread, bars of chocolate, tins of fish, sugar, and cooking oil. She keeps reminding me not to forget my promise. As we talk, she keeps taking off her sunglasses and putting them back on. I rummage in my handbag and hand her two banknotes.

"What are these for?" she asks.

"So you'll have some money of your own . . ."

"Ah . . . there's nothing much you can spend them on in the country . . . I'll keep them for the next time I'm here . . ."

"Do what you like with them, they're yours."

The bus drives away. I wave to her. She pretends to be crying and collecting the tears in her cupped hands. On the way back to the hostel I ask myself whether I did a good thing giving her that money. How can she not want to go to trades school? I realize that I just encouraged her.

Arriving at the hostel, I take out all my small change and count it. I'm almost broke. I ask Livia to lend me some money until payday.

Anyway, I still had to do everything I did, I tell myself calmly.

24

"Apostoae Emilia?" the secret policeman asks me, leafing through some documents.

I nod. He is a man of about forty, going slightly gray, with a placid face and a bored voice. I'd expected to see a harsher figure, with a thundering voice.

"Maiden name Burac?"

"Yes."

"Mother and father agricultural laborers?"

"Exactly."

"What does your husband do?"

"Locksmith mechanic."

"Yes . . . yes . . . But why aren't you a member of the Party?"

"Hmmm . . . I don't know . . . I don't think I have the required ideological level, comrade . . ."

"I see that you are a good element, you don't have any deviations . . ."

"That's right."

"You've been allocated a flat via the factory, how do you feel in it?"

"Good."

"Were you put forward for Party membership but turned down?"

"No."

"But if you were put forward, would you accept?"

"I don't know . . . I think so."

"And you say you don't have the required ideological level? How is that?"

"I don't know . . . That's what I think . . ."

"What are you lacking in order to have the necessary ideological level?"

"Perhaps I should study Party documents more . . . How should I know?"

"Are you satisfied with the collective you work in?"

"Yes."

"And with the foreman?"

"With him too."

"Do you have any complaints about the workplace?"

"Er, no."

"Do you consider that you lack anything in particular, which the factory might help you with?"

"I don't know . . . Maybe a gas canister . . ."

"Is that all?"

"Yes, I think so."

"Well then, fill in a request form, which you will leave with me, and tomorrow go to the union to pick up a voucher for the gas canister."

When I get back, they're on a break. I get out my packed lunch and sit on the bench outside, next to Aurelia.

"How was it?" she asks me.

I look at her amazed at how she knew.

"The boss told me that I have to go after the break as well."

"Aha," it all becomes clear to me. "He's all right, even so. He asks you what complaints you have. I told him that I'd like a gas canister and he told me to fill in a request form."

"But why hasn't he asked us up to now?"

I nod my head in sign that it's clear why now and not before. We eat. Finally, Aurelia gets out an orange. She tells me about how at her husband's shop they don't stint on unloading the goods. They get all kinds of stuff. Salami, milk, chocolate, everything. And not just them, but in almost all the neighborhoods. Well, there's still a line, but only twenty or thirty people, not hordes.

Maria comes over, so we stop talking. Aurelia offers her some of the opened orange. Maria takes a segment, picks off the pith, and then eats it. I look at her, my eyes bulging.

"I can't stand the pith. I eat oranges like grapefruit," she smiles.

So as not to show myself up, I don't tell her that I've not yet had occasion to eat a grapefruit.

In the afternoon, we all move on to outside. We sweep, clean, dig. We've received black earth, roses and pieces of lawn from the town hall. We paint all the outside pipes and the mobile crane. On the main wing of the factory, another team, from another section, paints in letters as tall as a man "Long Live the Romanian Communist Party." The porters have also been assigned two new colleagues. The asphalting of the road has reached the factory yard.

In the evening, when the power is cut off, they let us go home.

I get back exhausted. It's too late to phone Sanda to see how Alice is. I chat with Țucu for a little. We haven't spoken for two days. He tells me that they were taken off to transplant maize. They go to the Party Farm, uproot the maize from an experimental plot—large and comely maize, with great big cobs—and then they plant it at the edge of the fields, two or three rows deep, along the roads which Ceaușescu will travel down to I don't know what agricultural collective. They uproot the puny maize and load it into trailers. Even he doesn't know what happens after that. They carry out all these operations in the blazing sun. At least they give them mineral water.

The third day is a bit lighter. We're busy "decking out portraits." We divide into two teams, one for inside and one for outside. I'm inside. We make a panel of honor, with photographs of the foremost workers. We're having fun. We paste up Mitu's photograph as the best of the best, the model to be followed. Then we draw up a graph of political information meetings, with dates and topics that we just make up. That is, not exactly – we copy them from a template brought by the foreman. We cut out articles from newspapers, which we tack to a piece of polystyrene wrapped in red canvas. We hang up two or three portraits of Ceaușescu. The foreman brings us twenty thick volumes of the complete works of Uncle Nicu, to put in his office. Because he doesn't have a bookcase, we cart one from the Furniture Factory, on loan. He also brings forty flowerpots, for us to spread around the place, as aesthetically as possible. We have to sign for them. Whatever gets lost or broken, we'll have to pay for.

There's a hullabaloo outside. Someone's shouting.

Aurelia and me go to the door to see what it's all about.

A scowling guy with brown hair, wearing a suit and tie, is rolling his eyes and foaming at the mouth.

"You're a bunch of idiots and dolts! You're in for it now, I guarantee you! As soon as this visit is over you'll have me to answer to! Is this a factory for drunkards? Is it wine we make or do we produce for export? You're irresponsible."

And off he goes like a tornado, one of those ones that flatten everything in their path. We find out that it was the grapevines that had upset him. Mister Culidiuc is the most affected of all of us. He had planted them, cleaned them and trimmed them for years, and now the men have already set about pulling them up. He can't watch; he goes into the workshop. The foreman doesn't say anything, because the new workmates are there, but his eyes are blazing. I'll miss shade, too, the plump black bunches of grapes . . . Mister Culidiuc makes a sign to us that the scowling guy is barmy. We ask him who he is and he says that he is a bigwig in the County branch of the Party.

Not even an hour passes but the blond-haired young porter comes in guffawing. He wants to tell us something, but the foreman makes a discreet sign for him to be silent. The porter doesn't catch on and lets rip, thirteen to the dozen. He says that that guy just now—Comrade Tornado, as I've christened him in my mind—found fault with the pine trees by the main gate, and why are they so dusty. They explained to him that they had been washed with the hose, but that they couldn't get them any greener than that. Then the guy apparently began to bellow that he wasn't interested, that, if need be, they should paint them, only that they should look like real pine trees, from the mountains. And now, perched on the Electrical Plant trucks with mobile ladders, a number of men are painting the pine trees with spray guns.

Only Adrian, Maria and Mister Mitu laugh. Oh, and Mister Culidiuc, who is in the workshop, standing behind us.

Only now does the hapless porter understand. You can see by his frightened glance.

"In the end, it's one way of solving it," he tries to wriggle out of it.

This time, we all laugh.

The porter can't understand a thing.

The foreman takes him by the shoulders and asks him to show him where he saw such a thing, because he doesn't believe it. You can see from a mile off that he wants to get him out of the shit.

Today, we leave earlier, so that we'll have time to prepare for the next day and to have a rest. The foreman gives us our final instructions: overalls have to be ironed and starched; the men have to be shaven and to smell of toothpaste, not of rotgut; the woman shouldn't be wearing lipstick, makeup or nail varnish.

I get back home. Tucu isn't back yet. The pots are empty, and the sink is full. I get down to business. Tucu turns up. He tells me about how some chap with a loud mouth came and hauled them over the coals: them, for not watering the planted maize, and the guys from the Party Farm, who were getting ready a herd of thoroughbred cows to send to the agricultural collective that Ceaușescu was going to visit, for sabotaging the event. I described Tornado to him and he confirmed it was him. There had been a real carry-on with the cows. In the first place, he made them remove all the black cows from the herd, because they didn't lend an optimistic note. Then he was dissatisfied with the way they had been washed and curried. But the worst was when he battened onto their hooves, for not being glossy enough, because he knew that thoroughbred cows have to have shiny hooves. In the end, he made them lacquer the hooves, for them to look like in the textbook.

We go on chatting about this and that and then fall asleep.

The big day.

The director general and the foreman make the inspection. They closely examine each of us individually, straightening a collar or two. With all this protective gear on us we look like something out of an exhibition. The atmosphere is tense. Our new colleagues haven't turned up, probably because the official delegation has gone somewhere else. Comrade Suit goes out and we are left to ourselves. The time passes slowly. We walk to and fro, listlessly. We don't even feel like sitting down, so as not to crease anything.

On both sides of the street, workers, pioneers and communist youth have already been deployed, with placards and flags. Their chatter can be heard as far as in the factory yard.

From time to time, Mister Mitu walks around swaying, with arms outstretched, the way he imagines a cosmonaut walks. We smile, but we don't feel like laughing. Whatever you might say, we are excited. It's not every day that Ceaușescu comes to our workshop. And I think that we are a little afraid too, even if no one says so. We have to make a good impression! A very good impression!

From time to time, the foreman brings us news from Comrade Suit: Ceaușescu is in town; Ceaușescu is in the viewing stand, the parade is about to begin; Ceaușescu is having lunch; Ceaușescu is heading for the agricultural collective. The tension grows. The worst thing is that we don't have anything to do; we just have to wait. We have to be ready at any moment.

At around five in the afternoon, a stupendous piece of news arrives: Ceaușescu has left town.

But we remain in position, in case it's a false alarm.

At around seven, Comrade Suit appears and confirms that Ceaușescu has left town. He thanks us and tells us that maybe we will be luckier next time. He leaves in a hurry.

We're left to ourselves and the atmosphere suddenly relaxes. "Boss, what about those new colleagues of ours who didn't turn up today? What shall we do? Clock them out?" asks Mister Mitu drolly.

"Bugger them!"

We all decide to go to a restaurant and celebrate our achievement.

25

Mrs. Rozalia told her story in a whisper, with her eyes fixed on the old clock. From time to time she paused and gently urged me to have some more jam.

She was born in 1936. Her father owned a tailor's workshop and had three apprentices. Her mother was a housewife. She was an only child and very spoiled as a result. She liked to paint and still had drawings from when she was five or six years old. Little Rozalia's parents used to say she had talent and her mother encouraged her in that direction. Her father spent a lot of time at his workshop. He had a select and discerning clientele, which he didn't like to leave in the hands of his apprentices. All the town's notables ordered their clothes from Anton Buzinschi. Because he had a bad leg, her father was not called up during the war. Even during those difficult times, the family was quite well off. Little Rozalia started school and got very good marks. Drawing was by far her strongest point. The coming of communism spelled disaster for them. In 1949 the workshop was nationalized. Because her father had not taken part in the war, he was treated as an enemy of the people. He avoided being sent to prison thanks only to his relations with his former clientele. But overnight the family was thrown into poverty. They had barely anything to eat. They gave the best food to Rozalia. That meant bread and milk. With difficulty her mother managed to get a job as a seasonal worker at some greenhouses. When she came home from work, she had crippling pains in her back. Whatever job he applied for, her father was systematically rejected. Luckily, when he sensed the changes that were afoot

under the communists, her father had taken almost all his stock
of cloth and hidden it in the attic of a friend. He wasn't able to
salvage his sewing machines, however. And so in the early '50s
he used to sell bolts of cloth. Good quality cloth, in various colors, the likes of which you couldn't find in Romania. That attic
was little Rozalia's paradise. While her father selected the cloth,
she would stroke the bolts, smell them, unwind the material and
wrap herself up in it like a princess or a fairy. Later, she realized
that her father took her with him because it looked less suspi-
cious if he was with a small child. If they had caught him, nothing could have prevented him being sent to jail. It was highly
dangerous, but hunger impelled him to take the risk. He sold
the bolts of cloth at a quarter of the price to tailors, trustworthy
people he had known for a long time. The tailors used the cloth
to make suits for the elite of the new proletarian order.
Sometimes, on the street, her father would stop and point out a
dress to her: look, it's made from our cloth. It wasn't hard to spot
such clothes. The communists only produced brown, black and
grey cloth. The official colors were grey and navy blue. If our flag
weren't red, yellow and blue, we'd forget those colors existed, her
father used to say. Shoes were black or brown. Handbags and
umbrellas likewise. With the triumph of communism, the world
was reduced to two or three dark colors, like in a poor quality
photograph. People on the street looked like they were part of a
funeral procession. Little Rozalia grew up. She drew in pencil,
because watercolors were expensive. She still dreamed of becoming a painter. But in 1954, when, full of enthusiasm, she tried
to apply for university, her file was rejected. Once again, she
found out what it means to be a class enemy. They even gave her
moral homilies, so that she'd understand. Such children are
untrustworthy, because their parents have hostile attitudes. The
leopard doesn't change its spots. They mustn't hold positions of
responsibility in society. A university place taken by the child of
a bourgeois exploiter is a place stolen from the child of a proletarian, and so it isn't fair. She understood. She understood that
the comrades wouldn't let her be a painter. She wept, and with
difficulty she found a job as a cleaning lady in a state institution,

and then as a bus conductor. In 1958, as a result of sophisticated interventions, the regime did her father a favor: they gave him a job as a tailor, in the state-owned workshop that had once been his. His joy at having work was every day poisoned by the memories stirred by that workplace. The old sewing machines were still there. Of the old apprentices, only the clumsiest of them remained, but now he was the boss and a Party member. Fortunately, he didn't bear her father any grudge. And so in a short while Rozalia was given a job in the workshop. She learned how to be a seamstress. On learning that Anton Buzinschi had returned to work, many of his old customers returned. Almost nothing remained of the cloth in the clandestine storeroom. But it had done its duty, feeding the family for almost ten years. The only cloth left had partly rotted because of the damp. The bolts had lain in a place where rain leaked through the roof. In the '70s, the workshop was relocated, and the old building was converted into a small bookshop and then a food shop. It is still there, in the old quarter of town. After the Revolution, it changed hands a number of times and now it is a slot machine arcade. Her passion for painting never abandoned her. It was too late for her to make a career as a painter, but by way of compensation she taught drawing part-time at a school in the country. From time to time she painted landscapes. She gave up teaching because of the commute. It was tiring, it was cold, it was expensive. She spent almost all her wages on the bus fare. But she made a living as a seamstress. She liked what she did, but she suffered because of the colors. She was sick of brown, black and grey. It was like a holiday on the rare occasions when she could work with cherry-red, green or blue. Only the most courageous women had blue dresses made for themselves, since you could never find shoes or handbags to match.

"That, my dear, was communism for me: the communists confiscated my father's workshop, they shattered my dream of becoming a painter, they deprived me of colors all my life."

When the Revolution came, her father was seventy-four and almost blind. Like the good tailor he was and a man fearful of the times, he had saved some money. Some of it he kept in the national savings bank and some carefully hidden away at home, so that it would be handy. In December 1989 he wept: he'd never imagined that he would live to witness the fall of communism. Old and almost sightless, he'd gone out into the street, ready to offer his services to the forces of the Revolution. He had not had such a happy Christmas since he was a young man. He hoped with all his heart that those that had committed wrongs would be punished and that what they had stolen would be given back.

"As for colors, it's too late to repair that," said her father.

Then came the period of inflation. Father panicked. His life's savings were worth less and less with every passing month. The money you could have used to buy a car would now barely buy you a motorcycle. So, he decided to do something with his money. In desperation, he bought sewing machines. Ten of them. He stored them all in one room of his flat, where they took up all the space. He would have liked to set up another tailor's workshop, but he was too old. Two years later he died. Mrs. Rozalia wanted to fulfill his dream. The Liberals had promised to return the properties confiscated by the communists. From time to time, Mrs. Rozalia would go to the old quarter, enter the slot-machine arcade, and picture in her mind where she'd place the ten sewing machines. She was no longer able to work, but a few young people could bring the place back to life.

"Why didn't you ever tell me about this?" I asked her.

"I didn't think you would be interested . . ."

That evening, Alice phoned again to ask whether I had changed my mind. I think we must have talked for an hour on the phone. Ţucu was watching a film and kept dozing off. He was stocking up on sleep, because he was going to the country again the next day.

"Come on, Mother, I'll be a laughingstock at the association! What's the big deal? You just have to put an x in a different box!"

I told her that it was my life and I knew better what I had lived through. If everything was shit, then what about my youth? I hadn't done anybody any harm, I hadn't put anybody in prison, I hadn't been a secret police informer, so why should I feel guilty?

"It's not a question of guilt, Mother. It's just that you have to realize it was a bad system . . . unjust . . . even with the best intentions, it leads to ruin."

"Can't you put it more plainly?"

"In other words, even if you want to do good, you do harm. That's the way the system is. It's badly designed."

"How can the system be bad when I had a good life?"

"But what about others, Mother? What kind of life did other people have?"

"Other people . . . I'm 'other people' now, one of the ones who has a bad life. I'm voting for the times when other people were the other people."

"Wouldn't it be better if nobody was 'other people' anymore?"

"That I can agree with. That would be best."

"Then trust me."

"Would you look at that: the egg is teaching the hen!"

We bickered without any outcome. In the end, we reached the same conclusion as we had the last time: she has no reason to miss communism, whereas I have every reason to miss it.

"But we're still mother and daughter, aren't we?" joked Alice.

And I told her to take calcium, so that she wouldn't ruin her teeth.

"Cheese . . . cheese has calcium," muttered Țucu from the living room.

26

I'm in the one-room flat. It's been almost a year since I started renting it and I'm very happy. Not that it was bad at the hostel, I got on well with the other girls, but I didn't have a space of my own. I'm cooking up some pumpkin. In fact it's almost ready. The windows are open to let the smell out. I can hear the traffic outside, but it doesn't bother me too much. I put on a record. Last payday, I said to myself: that's it, you can't go on like this, you need a record player, Mica! And so I bought this one, which looks like a little valise. I thought that at a pinch I could take it with me to the country. I've started having things of my own. Now, if I move, a suitcase won't be enough, I'll have to take a taxi. Obviously, I bought a long soft towel for the bathroom, even if it was a bit pricey. I go back into the kitchen, lift the lid of the pan, sniff, prick the pumpkin with a fork. Just a little longer. I clear the table.

The doorbell rings.

I shrug. I'm not expecting anybody.

It's quite late.

I look through the spyhole and can't believe my eyes: Auntie Lucreția. I think that something bad must have happened at home.

"The next time you move, please tell me, my girl! I traipsed all the way to the hostel for nothing."

She is dressed all in white and wearing sunglasses.

"Come in, Auntie . . ." I mumble.

"It's quite big this flat of yours . . . Not bad at all!"

She puts her bag on the bed and sits down in the armchair.

From her casual tone of voice, she doesn't seem to have brought any bad news. I fetch her a glass of water and then nip back into the kitchen to check on the pumpkin. I turn the cooker off and come back. Auntie is leafing through a *Spark* almanac. Now she's taken her sunglasses off, a long bruise is visible under her right eye. I ask her whether she is hungry and she shakes her head. The record has finished, but I don't think it's the right moment to put on another.

Auntie asks me whether she can stay at my place overnight.

I tell her that she can sleep in the bed and I'll extend the armchair in which she's sitting.

I insist she try some pumpkin and she accepts.

"I'll bring it in here, Auntie, because the kitchen is too narrow for two bottoms."

I was trying to make a joke.

When I come back with the second plate, Auntie Lucreția is holding the photograph of Țucu. A small passport-size photograph.

"Who is he?"

"A boy . . ."

"I can see he's not a girl. What's his name?"

"Constantin."

"Is he your boyfriend?"

"Oh, Auntie . . . we've just been to the cinema a couple of times."

"He's quite a handsome boy . . . Look what eyes he's got! You ought to think about getting married . . ."

I sense I'm blushing and so I quickly go to fetch cutlery and napkins.

While Auntie is in the bathroom washing her hands, I hurriedly put the photograph in my purse.

That episode immediately brings to mind another, which happened ten years later.

It is late autumn and I've just arrived at my parents' on a visit. Father is picking beetroot, and Mother is busy doing chores. The same as always, I've brought them a few things. Besides bread, cooking oil and sugar, there are all kinds of things I received from the factory: a padded jacket, a pair of rubber boots, Cheia soap, soda. The same as always, Mother takes them to the shed, telling me not to bring anything else, because they don't have any use for them. For years and years I've been buying them firewood, so that they wouldn't have to make briquettes anymore, because they're old and frail, but they barely touch it. They refuse to give up treading manure. You can't wrench them out of their habits. It's as if they're always telling me that it's me they need, not the things I bring them.

Up until I got married, they still hoped that I would come back to the village. After the wedding they bid that hope farewell. In all the years that followed, I could feel their reproachful eyes boring into the back of my neck. They didn't say anything to me, but they had a way of looking at me that said it all. Father would look sidelong, as if he'd be forced to spill everything if he looked me straight in the eye. Mother would look at me sadly. Sadly and wearily. After Sanda went to vocational school, I thought that they would divide the blame equally. She took all the blame on herself, she didn't breathe a word about the help I'd given her. But no, it was all still on my shoulders, because to them Sanda had just copied what her older sister had done. As they got older, Father became sad and weary too, and Mother started to cry more and more often. My only defense, an indirect one, was always to show them that the future bore me out. After vocational school, I took lyceum courses at night school, even though I was satisfied with how much I was earning. I was terribly ambitious. I studied to take my university entrance exams. That was after I got married. I wanted to take a sub-engineering course, part time. I studied for two months for the exam, but I dropped everything when I found out I was pregnant. Alice arrived and I abandoned all my ambitions of getting into university. I packed my ambitions away in a satchel.

Mother dozes off more and more often when she sits down on a stool to catch her breath for a few minutes. She is snoring softly, leaning her head against the wall. Her hands are in her lap. I've constantly tried to make their lives easier, but they receive my gestures without any joy. I've repaired the house, the well, I got them electricity, but the reproach still glitters in their eyes. I'm accustomed to it by now.

I nip out into the garden. I take a deep breath of autumn air. The heaps of pumpkins, with their orange aureoles, seem to light up everything around them. The hoods of the corncobs rustle in the breeze. In the tree, I glimpse a few apples. I manage to reach one. They are small and sweet. Sometimes it's very nice in the country. Especially when you're only visiting. I toss the apple core in the sty, but the pig doesn't bother with it.

I hear voices and so I go back to the house. Father has come back, with a pitchfork resting on his shoulder. Mother has woken up and is boiling some maize porridge. We sit down on the stools next to the outdoor stove. We talk. The old man is out of sorts. I ask him what's wrong, but he waves his hand, it's nothing good and he doesn't feel like talking about it.

"Haven't you heard?" asks Mother.

"No. Heard what?"

"About how your Uncle Andrei's gone mad."

"How so? What did he do?"

"Let your father tell you."

The old man reluctantly tells the story. I find out that Uncle Andrei has run away with a woman thirty years younger than him. Auntie Lucreţia kicked up a storm. There was a Party meeting and they kicked him out of his job, for inappropriate behavior. But they didn't take back his membership card.

We fall silent. There is nothing else to say.

I'm amazed at how the news reaches the village more quickly, even if things happen farther away.

"The man's mad," mutters Father.

I say neither yes nor no.

27

INSIDE IT SMELLS vaguely of pinewood and strongly of glue. In the large meeting room on the ground floor of the Trade Unions Building there are around twenty of us and I only know one or two to look at. We are making placards for an urgent demonstration. The slogans were delivered to us right from the start: "Down with the Timişoara hooligans!" "We demand law and order in the land!" We already have plenty of placards saying things like "Long live the Romanian Communist Party" and "Ceauşescu, Romania, our hope and pride," and all we need to do is touch up a few of the letters. I was summoned by Dorofte, the Party secretary at our factory, who is also responsible for the entire operation. The people I know to look at are also from our factory. I don't know whether Dorofte summoned me to take revenge or whether this is the rule: that new Party members have to do chores like this.

When I joined the Party, less than a year ago, the secretary was all sweetness and light, but following an incident, he no longer sees me in a good light.

This is what happened.

It was the first day of Easter and we were all in the workshop. I'd told the foreman that we were Orthodox and that we couldn't work at Easter. The foreman didn't have any objection, on the condition that we made up the hours. Early that morning, we turned on a few of the machines and laid out the Easter repast: sweet cheese pie, painted eggs, *cozonac*, wine. We would celebrate somehow, even if we weren't at home. The atmosphere was pleasant, we chatted, we told jokes, we were having a good time in our own way. Around lunchtime, the doorbell rang, but without our secret code. We looked at each other and went on the alert. We cleared the table, put everything in the cupboard and took up stations at the machines. It took a little while before we opened the door. It was Dorofte. He didn't say anything, he started walking around the workshop and looking in every nook and cranny. I think there must have been a smell of wine and boiled eggs, even if we didn't realize it. Then he started looking in the rubbish bin and found what he was probably looking for: painted eggshells. We hadn't anticipated that.

"How did these get here?" he asked, looking at us triumphantly.

Nobody said anything.

"I asked you something," said Dorofte. Then he added: "Comrade Apostaoe, you recently joined the Party. Do you think it is good what is happening here?"

I looked at my feet.

"Please come to the table so that we can write out a statement. Something like this cannot go unpunished," he said, addressing me.

I looked for a piece of paper and a pen and then I sat down to write what he dictated. I was on the verge of tears.

Probably somebody had informed the foreman, because I hadn't even finished writing the statement when he showed up. Dorofte stiffly explained the situation.

"Yes, comrade, I'm sure you're right. But it's just a tradition, you know how it is . . . It's not necessarily religious feeling . . . And on their lunch break, comrade, they're allowed to eat whatever they've brought from home, whatever their wives or mother-in-laws put in their packed lunches," said the foreman, smoothing things over.

He was a big diplomat, that foreman of ours! Otherwise he wouldn't have got where he did.

But Dorofte was still quarrelsome, he demanded we all sign the written statement. We looked at the foreman and he nodded.

After that they went inside the office.

I don't know what the foreman told him, how he tricked him, but after a while he stuck his head out of the door and gave us a well-known signal. The signal to bring something good to drink. He always had coffee and cigarettes in his office. We brought him the best brandy we could lay our hands on, because there was nowhere we could get whiskey so fast. That was already a good sign. Two hours later, he signaled us to bring another bottle. In other words, the problem had been solved.

But we were no longer in the mood. It was time to knock off work, but nobody felt like going home. We were waiting to see what would happen in the end and to get a ticking off from the foreman.

Around five o'clock, they came out of the office. Both of them were tottering. The foreman wasn't a big drinker, but when he had to get drunk, he'd do it. This time he hadn't had any choice. As he was walking out of the door, taking Dorofte to a waiting taxi, he handed me the written statement. I tore it to shreds and threw it in the bin.

He came back, collected his things, and told us in a thick voice:

"We'll talk tomorrow."

Ever since then, I've been trying to avoid Dorofte. Now that we're in the same room, it's harder. Every time he passes, I pretend to be concentrating on what I'm doing. Yesterday I went to the Party meeting. It was a big one, for the whole factory. At the end, Dorofte personally assigned me to the team preparing the placards. It was an unusual meeting, at which they condemned the hooligans in Timişoara. Ţucu, who listens to Free Europe, had told me what it was about. It was an uprising and the army were shooting at the population. It was worse than Braşov in '87. Students had been sent home at four o'clock, to prevent them from demonstrating, and so Alice was at home. That made me feel a little calmer. I think everybody in the room knew what was happening, because the atmosphere was quite tense. Dorofte was inflamed. He fulminated against the destabilizing forces and urged us to do everything to preserve the conquests made by communism. The other speakers, although they talked along the same lines, had been somewhat calmer. After that other people got up on the podium to condemn the stone-age behavior of the people in Timișoara and express their support for the firm measures taken by the Party.

Dorofte walks among us and urges us to hurry.

I'm cutting a letter 'm' out of some polystyrene. Others are fastening red cloth to the wooden frames that have arrived from the carpentry shop. I've been given some long strips of fake leather, full of 'm's' traced in pencil, which I have to cut out. To speed things up, each person has been given a single letter. That's so you don't get mixed up and so you start to make the same movements automatically. As we cut out the letters, other people start gluing them to the cloth. The 'm's' are an easy job, because there are not that many of them. The people doing the 'i's' have got the worst job, because there are lots of 'i's.' The 'd's' are the easiest of all, because the only one is in "Down." The 't's' as well, as in "Timișoara."

Somebody appears in the doorway and shouts:

"Ceaușescu has been deposed! The dictator has fled"

We stop work and stare at him, astounded, as if he were mentally ill.

"Come quickly, it's on the television! Come and see!"

We all crowd toward the door.

I don't know where the television is, but I follow the others. They're saying something about a dictator, about a criminal and about freedom.

Joy! Everybody is hugging each other. But not Dorofte, who has vanished.

What is Țucu doing? What is Alice doing?

I run home, happy and frightened.

In the evening we go into the center of town. There is a crowd of people, waving flags with holes cut out of the center. People are giving speeches from a balcony. The crowd is chanting slogans. Finally, we go home, to watch events on television.

"In any case, it's more important what's happening in Bucharest than here in our small town," says Țucu.

28

SANDA LIVES AT the other end of town, and so I set out an hour earlier. As regards my great plan to bring the past back to life, I was no longer so sure about it. I told myself that maybe it would be better to test the waters first and then bring up the subject. Otherwise I ran the risk of it coming to nothing. All the same, I thought, I couldn't just spring it on them, without preparing them for it. I put a cake in a plastic bag and went to the tram stop. Lord, how much the price of a ticket had gone up! Almost twice what a monthly wage was under Ceaușescu. I got off at the station and continued on foot. She'd moved there about five years ago. They had sold their flat and bought a house with a small back garden. They weren't doing very well, but they tried to survive on what they managed to grow in the garden. Silviu, her husband, had cobbled together a little carpentry workshop, where he fixed things for people from the local area, but he didn't do all that much, since he was getting old. They'd bought the house at a good price, from a family that was moving to the country. The people who sold the house had had some misfortune or other with their daughter, who had run off with a motorcyclist, and so to make ends meet and because they were now the shame of the street, they'd gone back to the village, to his parents', who apparently had a great big farm. Sanda was happy. She said it was like being in the country and in the town at the same time, but I thought it was like neither the country nor the town. I'd only visited her two or three times. The last time had been about three months ago. We kept in touch over the phone.

It was as if the street had changed since the last time I'd been there. All kinds of new houses had gone up, painted yellow or blue, like hotels at the seaside. Probably bigwigs from town looking for cleaner air. They had gardens with flowers—not a trace of cabbages or parsley—paths with flagstones, and Alsatians poking their muzzles through the wrought iron gates. One of the villas even had a little fountain, in which two children were splashing around. Up until three years ago there had only been the Colonel's house, as Sanda called it, but now another four great big villas had sprung up, five even. True, most of them were near the end of the street by the station, not down the hill, near the shop, where Sanda's house was. But in a few years it wasn't out of the question that more villas would pop up next to her house, villas with big-bellied men sunning themselves in the garden. Sanda said it was as if she'd moved overnight to the Ivory Coast, instead of the edge of a dusty small town. If I thought about it, the house that Ceauşescu built for himself back then, the one that we thought looked like a palace, was like a hut compared to all the villas springing up all over the place now, like mushrooms after the rain. I'd never have thought that so much building could go on in that corner of town next to the fields.

We kissed each other and hugged. Sanda had brought the table and a few chairs outside, under the walnut tree. It was nice there, in the open air. My sister looked well, and the house was completely changed, having been renovated. The plant pots lined up on the porch lent the house a holiday feeling. I measured up the yard with my eyes and it seemed to me just right for a factory. A small one, for starters.

"This is Luş, Silviu found him somewhere or other . . . A house isn't a house unless there's a dog to wag its tail . . ."

The dog seemed timid. It hid behind Sanda's dressing gown like a small child. It was a mongrel, but it had perky ears and eyes as big and as round as walnuts. It was nice. Silviu wasn't at home, and so it would be just us girls.

"Where's Aurelia?" I ask.

"She phoned to say she would be late. She has to finish doing something at the shop."

In the meantime, my sister brought me up to date about Aurelia. I learned that she and my sister had been seeing each other more often, since our former workmate lived not far away, somewhere near the station. They were around the same age, about five years younger than me, but we all left the factory at the same time, when they locked the gates once and for all. Aurelia had opened a little shop, selling everything. Her husband had worked in a storeroom all his life and so running a shop was something he was used to. He had to go back and forth all day, but he didn't complain. Her son-in-law had a bakery in a nearby village and he supplied them with bread. They got the rest of their wares from the wholesaler's. They'd bought a car. Even Sanda bought from their shop, when she was passing. They had good prices. Whenever they bumped into each other, they stopped for a chat. But never for long, because Aurelia was always busy because of the shop. It's not a bad thing that they are managing, I told myself: they could provide financial support to get the plan off the ground.

"Hey, it's starting to look like in town around here!" called Aurelia, coming through the gate like a whirlwind.

"Well, what did you expect?"

Aurelia was wearing a linen blouse with puffy sleeves, a chic skirt and high-soled sandals. She was wearing sunglasses. He gait was just as heavy as ever and her mouth just as loud.

"You look like you've put on a little weight, but it suits you!" I said, getting up off my chair and giving her a hug.

"Hmm, I've put on a few kilos . . . It's the stress . . . But that's it, I'm going on a diet! Salad or whatnot for lunch and fruit in the evening . . ."

She took some cakes out of her bag, a two-liter bottle of juice, and a bunch of bananas. She put everything on the table, next to the slices of my cake.

"Ta-da! And now for the surprise," she said, producing a bottle. "We'll have a little sip of this, since we haven't seen each other since I don't know when. That's why I didn't come in the car . . ."

It was whiskey cream. I'd never drunk it before.

The three of us sat around the table and we started chatting. Luş was still hiding behind Sanda's dressing gown. All I could see was his tail twitching. Aurelia was talking about her granddaughter:

"She's a handful, I'm telling you! Everybody says she takes after me. The truth is, she looks a bit like me. Before she gave birth, my daughter-in-law didn't view me very well. You know what they say: the child looks like the person the mother's got a grudge against . . ."

"Back in Ceauşescu's day, it was different bringing up a child. I wouldn't have one now . . ."

"Our little'un has got everything she could possibly want, on my word!"

"I miss those days, to be honest. Can you remember what fun we used to have in the workshop . . . what a life that was," I said, almost in tears.

Sanda knew my opinion about it, and so she wasn't surprised. But Aurelia stared at me and then said:

"Are you serious?"

"Do I look like I'm joking?"

"Well, what can I say . . . In a way, I wasn't as rushed as I am now, I wasn't as busy . . ."

Sanda jumped up, knocking Luş onto his back so his legs were in the air. She hurried inside. The phone was ringing.

"Not as rushed, and with a fridge full of food!" I added.

"The truth is that compared with the poverty around us, we lived like boyars . . . Because we worked for export. Otherwise . . . otherwise, you'd have seen how long we'd have had to wait in line."

"Remember the beers and the juice in the bathtub?"

"We were mad. As mad as can be!"

"Backgammon, dice, cards . . ."

"The only thing we didn't have was a roulette wheel!"

"Remember when you beat them in the backgammon championship?"

"Do I! Lord, I gave them a drubbing! Me, a woman, and I thrashed them . . . I played Ariton in the final. They were all rooting for him, the bastards! We all got really fired up . . ."

"Heard anything from Ariton?"

"Nothing much . . . I met him a few years ago. He'd got a job with a private company, but didn't know how long it would last . . ."

"What about that idiot Dragoş?"

"Oho, he's a real big wheel now, has his own wine wholesaler's. I'd like to have a business like that . . ."

"That good-for-nothing has really done that well for himself?"

"And how! I think his uncle had a hand in it, the former Party secretary . . . All the ex-communists are big businessmen now."

"Really?" I said, in amazement.

"That's what you hear . . . Most of the ex-communists are capitalists now. What, didn't you know? They're everywhere you look. Although I came across one where you'd least expect . . . Guess where?"

"I don't know . . . go on, tell me!"

"In a monastery."

"You don't say!"

"I'm telling you . . . I was there a year ago, with the whole family. All kinds of monks going about their business. So, I go to buy an icon and the monk who's selling them looks familiar. Where have I seen him before? I ask myself."

"Who was it?"

"Hold your horses! So, where have I seen him before? I turned around and took another look. The monk gave me a smile. A pious smile, the way they do. He was quite elderly . . . And all of a sudden it comes to me: Dorofte!"

"You're kidding! Dorofte?"

"Hold your horses! I couldn't believe it either, I thought I must have made a mistake . . . So, I went up to him and asked:

you? That's all I asked. He nodded. It was him! The Party secretary from the factory, selling icons, can you imagine?"

"I can't believe it . . ."

"It took me two days to get over it . . . You should have seen
what a gentle face he had!"

"He was the one who made me join the Party."

"Now it's you who ought to go and lend him a helping hand,"
said Aurelia and laughed heartily.

Sanda came back, flushed, carrying a bucket of water. In her
other hand she was holding a cup.

"Water from the well, if you'd like some . . ."

"We were talking about the people we used to work with," I
said, bringing her up to date on the conversation. "Do you know
who Aurelia saw?"

"She knows about Dorofte, I told her . . ."

"Why didn't you tell me?" I asked my sister reproachfully.

"I forgot."

"Have you heard anything about Mister Mitu?" I asked, looking now at one, now at the other.

"When I moved here," began Sanda, "I used to see him walking down the hill. He used to go to a kind of tavern, which they
called the Crumpled Tractor, which was where the food kiosk is
now. About two years after I moved, the tavern closed and they
opened that shop. It's good, because they have most of everything. Ah, yes, I was telling you about Mister Mitu . . . I used
to go there and tell those stories of his and they'd all be rolling
around with laughter."

"Caught you!" said Aurelia. "Neither of you read the papers,
do you?"

"Not really, they're too expensive," admitted Sanda.

I didn't read them for the same reason.

"You're fusty old pensioners who've got no idea what's going
on around town. Mister Mitu is standing for election on the
council!"

"Get out of here! You've caught the disease off him and now
you're telling tall tales," I said, skeptically.

"I'm telling you! But that's old news. Let me tell you the real bombshell. I read it in the paper the other day . . ."

"Another tall tale?" I snapped.

"No, honest! It isn't a tall tale about Mister Mitu standing for election either. He's standing for the Greater Romania Party, near the bottom of the list, he doesn't stand much of a chance, but he's there . . ."

"What's the bombshell?" asked Sanda.

"Well, the bombshell is that a journalist has published a list of all the candidates who were secret police informers, and Mister Mitu's one of them."

"I don't believe it. How did that journalist know?" I said, getting annoyed.

"I don't know how he knows, confidential sources, but I can believe that Mister Mitu was capable of it."

"So, now they were all informers . . . I don't know . . . I just can't believe it . . . Don't you remember how many jokes about Ceauşescu he used to tell?"

"Why do you think he never got into trouble?" said my sister.

"Well, didn't you ever tell a joke about Ceauşescu? Did anything ever happen to you?" I said.

"Sanda told jokes only every now and then, whereas Mister Mitu . . ." said Aurelia coming to her defense.

I think we must have talked about Mister Mitu for almost an hour, until we all decided we had better change the subject. There were still so many other things to discuss . . .

The whiskey cream was good stuff, no mistake, but after two glasses I was overwhelmed with melancholy . . . I was getting more and more weepy, but Aurelia was getting more and more raucous, and I didn't even dare think about my plan. When communism came up, Sanda always used to say that the dead don't come back from the grave and that she was happy with what she had.

"But Aurelia, we were happy . . ." I said for the umpteenth time.

"Rubbish! We did have food, true, but were we happy? I'm happier now, even when I get home in the evening worn out . . . It was a stupid regime."

"But we didn't even care . . . We used to laugh at it, don't you remember?"

"We used to laugh to forget about our sorrows."

"But we used to have fun, we felt good together . . ."

"You know what it's like when you laugh to forget about your sorrows? You can't be bothered, but someone comes and tickles you by force. You laugh because you haven't got any choice, but that doesn't mean you're over the moon with happiness . . ."

"And what a foreman we had . . ."

"Right, what a foreman. A lecher and a black marketer . . . He made a fortune from our labor . . . And I'm not even going to tell you how many times he came on to me . . ."

"You won't admit anything! Look at what's happened to the factories. Is that what they looked like back then? Nowadays, if you want to take home a pot of paint or a bit of pipe . . ."

"You know what, Mica? If the girls at my shop stole like we did from the factory, I'd be bankrupt in two weeks . . ."

"I didn't mean it like that, because there was plenty."

"And I've got plenty."

"All right, but that's different . . ."

"Right, it's as if somebody took something from my house. It's mine."

"I meant that I miss those days . . . I miss them . . . tears come to my eyes when I think about it."

"So why aren't you crying?"

"I am crying!"

And I really did start to cry.

I was crying for those times, but also because Aurelia, whom I'd worked with for twenty years, didn't want to admit how happy we'd all been. Because Lord God, her memories were so different than mine . . . Because I sensed that sometimes she was right. Because I'd come up with a wonderful plan and she didn't give me an opportunity to share it.

29

I HAD FORGOTTEN that Ţucu was away in the country and so I was disappointed to find the house empty. It would have done me good to have somebody to chat with. I tried to watch a film, but I wasn't interested in anything that was happening on the screen. Those people had lives that didn't resemble mine one little bit. It was stupid, but I was envious. What business of mine was it what they did, if they weren't interested in what I did? I turned off the television and started vacuuming the floor. As it was quite late by then, a neighbor started banging on the radiator and so I stopped.

I sat down on the bed and thought about the visit that afternoon.

That conversation with Aurelia hadn't been at all to my liking. I was out of sorts.

I felt how my past was starting to change. There were new pieces that didn't fit the puzzle, forcing me to start the game all over again. Other memories came back to me. Gestures and feelings I had forgotten. The same places, the same people, the same time, but different events. Aurelia shouldn't have done what she did. We had all been one family and up until recently we had all been happy. But now . . . now it was beginning to unravel.

And then there was Sanda, who hadn't said anything . . .

Since when had my sister viewed me as a communist old biddy? Why were our memories so different? How many happy people do you need around you to be happy yourself?

Finally, I fell asleep.

Tomorrow? Yes, the elections are tomorrow . . .

I think I'll just sit quietly at home and I'll . . . and I'll find something to keep me busy.

DAN LUNGU is one of the most important Romanian novelists to have emerged in the post-communist period. His award-winning novels, which include *Hens' Heaven, How to Forget a Woman, In Hell All the Light Bulbs are Burnt Out*, and *The Little Girl Who Played at Being God*, have been translated into almost every European language, as well as having been made into feature films and adapted for the stage.

ALISTAIR IAN BLYTH, a native of Sunderland, England, has resided for many years in Bucharest. Among his previous translations are: *The Bulgarian Truck* by Dumitru Tsepeneag, *The Encounter* by Gabriela Adameşteanu (both available from Dalkey Archive Press), *Miruna* by Bogdan Suceavă, and *An Intellectual History of Cannibalism* by Cătălin Avramescu.

MICHAL AJVAZ, *The Golden Age.*
The Other City.

PIERRE ALBERT-BIROT, *Grabinoulor.*

YUZ ALESHKOVSKY, *Kangaroo.*

FELIPE ALFAU, *Chromos.*
Locos.

JOE AMATO, *Samuel Taylor's Last Night.*

IVAN ÂNGELO, *The Celebration.*
The Tower of Glass.

ANTÓNIO LOBO ANTUNES, *Knowledge of Hell.*
The Splendor of Portugal.

ALAIN ARIAS-MISSON, *Theatre of Incest.*

JOHN ASHBERY & JAMES SCHUYLER, *A Nest of Ninnies.*

ROBERT ASHLEY, *Perfect Lives.*

GABRIELA AVIGUR-ROTEM, *Heatwave and Crazy Birds.*

DJUNA BARNES, *Ladies Almanack.*
Ryder.

JOHN BARTH, *Letters.*
Sabbatical.

DONALD BARTHELME, *The King.*
Paradise.

SVETISLAV BASARA, *Chinese Letter.*

MIQUEL BAUÇÀ, *The Siege in the Room.*

RENÉ BELLETTO, *Dying.*

MAREK BIEŃCZYK, *Transparency.*

ANDREI BITOV, *Pushkin House.*

ANDREJ BLATNIK, *You Do Understand.*
Law of Desire.

LOUIS PAUL BOON, *Chapel Road.*
My Little War.
Summer in Termuren.

ROGER BOYLAN, *Killoyle.*

IGNÁCIO DE LOYOLA BRANDÃO, *Anonymous Celebrity.*
Zero.

BONNIE BREMSER, *Troia: Mexican Memoirs.*

CHRISTINE BROOKE-ROSE, *Amalgamemnon.*

BRIGID BROPHY, *In Transit.*
The Prancing Novelist.

GERALD L. BRUNS, *Modern Poetry and the Idea of Language.*

GABRIELLE BURTON, *Heartbreak Hotel.*

MICHEL BUTOR, *Degrees.*
Mobile.

G. CABRERA INFANTE, *Infante's Inferno.*
Three Trapped Tigers.

JULIETA CAMPOS, *The Fear of Losing Eurydice.*

ANNE CARSON, *Eros the Bittersweet.*

ORLY CASTEL-BLOOM, *Dolly City.*

LOUIS-FERDINAND CÉLINE, *North.*
Conversations with Professor Y.
London Bridge.

MARIE CHAIX, *The Laurels of Lake Constance.*

HUGO CHARTERIS, *The Tide Is Right.*

ERIC CHEVILLARD, *Demolishing Nisard.*
The Author and Me.

MARC CHOLODENKO, *Mordechai Schamz.*

JOSHUA COHEN, *Witz.*

EMILY HOLMES COLEMAN, *The Shutter of Snow.*

ERIC CHEVILLARD, *The Author and Me.*

ROBERT COOVER, *A Night at the Movies.*

STANLEY CRAWFORD, *Log of the S.S. The Mrs Unguentine.*
Some Instructions to My Wife.

RENÉ CREVEL, *Putting My Foot in It.*

RALPH CUSACK, *Cadenza.*

NICHOLAS DELBANCO, *Sherbrookes.*
The Count of Concord.

NIGEL DENNIS, *Cards of Identity.*

PETER DIMOCK, *A Short Rhetoric for Leaving the Family.*

ARIEL DORFMAN, *Konfidenz.*

COLEMAN DOWELL, *Island People.*
Too Much Flesh and Jabez.

ARKADII DRAGOMOSHCHENKO, *Dust.*

RIKKI DUCORNET, *Phosphor in Dreamland.*
The Complete Butcher's Tales.

RIKKI DUCORNET (cont.), *The Jade Cabinet.*
The Fountains of Neptune.

WILLIAM EASTLAKE, *The Bamboo Bed.*
Castle Keep.
Lyric of the Circle Heart.

JEAN ECHENOZ, *Chopin's Move.*

STANLEY ELKIN, *A Bad Man.*
Criers and Kibitzers, Kibitzers and Criers.
The Dick Gibson Show.
The Franchiser.
The Living End.
Mrs. Ted Bliss.

FRANÇOIS EMMANUEL, *Invitation to a Voyage.*

PAUL EMOND, *The Dance of a Sham.*

SALVADOR ESPRIU, *Ariadne in the Grotesque Labyrinth.*

LESLIE A. FIEDLER, *Love and Death in the American Novel.*

JUAN FILLOY, *Op Oloop.*

ANDY FITCH, *Pop Poetics.*

GUSTAVE FLAUBERT, *Bouvard and Pécuchet.*

KASS FLEISHER, *Talking out of School.*

JON FOSSE, *Aliss at the Fire.*
Melancholy.

FORD MADOX FORD, *The March of Literature.*

MAX FRISCH, *I'm Not Stiller.*
Man in the Holocene.

CARLOS FUENTES, *Christopher Unborn.*
Distant Relations.
Terra Nostra.
Where the Air Is Clear.

TAKEHIKO FUKUNAGA, *Flowers of Grass.*

WILLIAM GADDIS, JR., *The Recognitions.*

JANICE GALLOWAY, *Foreign Parts.*
The Trick Is to Keep Breathing.

WILLIAM H. GASS, *Life Sentences.*
The Tunnel.
The World Within the Word.
Willie Masters' Lonesome Wife.

GÉRARD GAVARRY, *Hoppla! 1 2 3.*

ETIENNE GILSON, *The Arts of the Beautiful.*
Forms and Substances in the Arts.

C. S. GISCOMBE, *Giscome Road.*
Here.

DOUGLAS GLOVER, *Bad News of the Heart.*

WITOLD GOMBROWICZ, *A Kind of Testament.*

PAULO EMÍLIO SALES GOMES, *P's Three Women.*

GEORGI GOSPODINOV, *Natural Novel.*

JUAN GOYTISOLO, *Count Julian.*
Juan the Landless.
Makbara.
Marks of Identity.

HENRY GREEN, *Blindness.*
Concluding.
Doting.
Nothing.

JACK GREEN, *Fire the Bastards!*

JIŘÍ GRUŠA, *The Questionnaire.*

MELA HARTWIG, *Am I a Redundant Human Being?*

JOHN HAWKES, *The Passion Artist.*
Whistlejacket.

ELIZABETH HEIGHWAY, ED., *Contemporary Georgian Fiction.*

AIDAN HIGGINS, *Balcony of Europe.*
Blind Man's Bluff.
Bornholm Night-Ferry.
Langrishe, Go Down.
Scenes from a Receding Past.

KEIZO HINO, *Isle of Dreams.*

KAZUSHI HOSAKA, *Plainsong.*

ALDOUS HUXLEY, *Antic Hay.*
Point Counter Point.
Those Barren Leaves.
Time Must Have a Stop.

NAOYUKI II, *The Shadow of a Blue Cat.*

DRAGO JANČAR, *The Tree with No Name.*

MIKHEIL JAVAKHISHVILI, *Kvachi.*

GERT JONKE, *The Distant Sound.*
Homage to Czerny.
The System of Vienna.

JACQUES JOUET, *Mountain R.*
 Savage.
 Upstaged.
MIEKO KANAI, *The Word Book.*
YORAM KANIUK, *Life on Sandpaper.*
ZURAB KARUMIDZE, *Dagny.*
JOHN KELLY, *From Out of the City.*
HUGH KENNER, *Flaubert, Joyce and Beckett: The Stoic Comedians.*
 Joyce's Voices.
DANILO KIŠ, *The Attic.*
 The Lute and the Scars.
 Psalm 44.
 A Tomb for Boris Davidovich.
ANITA KONKKA, *A Fool's Paradise.*
GEORGE KONRÁD, *The City Builder.*
TADEUSZ KONWICKI, *A Minor Apocalypse.*
 The Polish Complex.
ANNA KORDZAIA-SAMADASHVILI, *Me, Margarita.*
MENIS KOUMANDAREAS, *Koula.*
ELAINE KRAF, *The Princess of 72nd Street.*
JIM KRUSOE, *Iceland.*
AYSE KULIN, *Farewell: A Mansion in Occupied Istanbul.*
EMILIO LASCANO TEGUI, *On Elegance While Sleeping.*
ERIC LAURRENT, *Do Not Touch.*
VIOLETTE LEDUC, *La Bâtarde.*
EDOUARD LEVÉ, *Autoportrait.*
 Newspaper.
 Suicide.
 Works.
MARIO LEVI, *Istanbul Was a Fairy Tale.*
DEBORAH LEVY, *Billy and Girl.*
JOSÉ LEZAMA LIMA, *Paradiso.*
ROSA LIKSOM, *Dark Paradise.*
OSMAN LINS, *Avalovara.*
 The Queen of the Prisons of Greece.
FLORIAN LIPUŠ, *The Errors of Young Tjaž.*
GORDON LISH, *Peru.*
ALF MACLOCHLAINN, *Out of Focus.*
 Past Habitual.

 The Corpus in the Library.
RON LOEWINSOHN, *Magnetic Field(s).*
YURI LOTMAN, *Non-Memoirs.*
D. KEITH MANO, *Take Five.*
MINA LOY, *Stories and Essays of Mina Loy.*
MICHELINE AHARONIAN MARCOM,
 A Brief History of Yes.
 The Mirror in the Well.
BEN MARCUS, *The Age of Wire and String.*
WALLACE MARKFIELD, *Teitlebaum's Window.*
DAVID MARKSON, *Reader's Block.*
 Wittgenstein's Mistress.
CAROLE MASO, *AVA.*
HISAKI MATSUURA, *Triangle.*
LADISLAV MATEJKA & KRYSTYNA POMORSKA, EDS., *Readings in Russian Poetics: Formalist & Structuralist Views.*
HARRY MATHEWS, *Cigarettes.*
 The Conversions.
 The Human Country.
 The Journalist.
 My Life in CIA.
 Singular Pleasures.
 The Sinking of the Odradek.
 Stadium.
 Tlooth.
HISAKI MATSUURA, *Triangle.*
DONAL MCLAUGHLIN, *beheading the virgin mary, and other stories.*
JOSEPH MCELROY, *Night Soul and Other Stories.*
ABDELWAHAB MEDDEB, *Talismano.*
GERHARD MEIER, *Isle of the Dead.*
HERMAN MELVILLE, *The Confidence-Man.*
AMANDA MICHALOPOULOU, *I'd Like.*
STEVEN MILLHAUSER, *The Barnum Museum.*
 In the Penny Arcade.
RALPH J. MILLS, JR., *Essays on Poetry.*
MOMUS, *The Book of Jokes.*
CHRISTINE MONTALBETTI, *The Origin of Man.*
 Western.

NICHOLAS MOSLEY, *Accident*.
Assassins.
Catastrophe Practice.
A Garden of Trees.
Hopeful Monsters.
Imago Bird.
Inventing God.
Look at the Dark.
Metamorphosis.
Natalie Natalia.
Serpent.

WARREN MOTTE, *Fables of the Novel: French Fiction since 1990*.
Fiction Now: The French Novel in the 21st Century.
Mirror Gazing.
Oulipo: A Primer of Potential Literature.

GERALD MURNANE, *Barley Patch*.
Inland.

YVES NAVARRE, *Our Share of Time*.
Sweet Tooth.

DOROTHY NELSON, *In Night's City*.
Tar and Feathers.

ESHKOL NEVO, *Homesick*.

WILFRIDO D. NOLLEDO, *But for the Lovers*.

BORIS A. NOVAK, *The Master of Insomnia*.

FLANN O'BRIEN, *At Swim-Two-Birds*.
The Best of Myles.
The Dalkey Archive.
The Hard Life.
The Poor Mouth.
The Third Policeman.

CLAUDE OLLIER, *The Mise-en-Scène*.
Wert and the Life Without End.

PATRIK OUŘEDNÍK, *Europeana*.
The Opportune Moment, 1855.

BORIS PAHOR, *Necropolis*.

FERNANDO DEL PASO, *News from the Empire*.
Palinuro of Mexico.

ROBERT PINGET, *The Inquisitory*.
Mahu or The Material.
Trio.

MANUEL PUIG, *Betrayed by Rita Hayworth*.

The Buenos Aires Affair.
Heartbreak Tango.

RAYMOND QUENEAU, *The Last Days*.
Odile.
Pierrot Mon Ami.
Saint Glinglin.

ANN QUIN, *Berg*.
Passages.
Three.
Tripticks.

ISHMAEL REED, *The Free-Lance Pallbearers*.
The Last Days of Louisiana Red.
Ishmael Reed: The Plays.
Juice!
The Terrible Threes.
The Terrible Twos.
Yellow Back Radio Broke-Down.

JASIA REICHARDT, *15 Journeys Warsaw to London*.

JOÃO UBALDO RIBEIRO, *House of the Fortunate Buddhas*.

JEAN RICARDOU, *Place Names*.

RAINER MARIA RILKE,
The Notebooks of Malte Laurids Brigge.

JULIÁN RÍOS, *The House of Ulysses*.
Larva: A Midsummer Night's Babel.
Poundemonium.

ALAIN ROBBE-GRILLET, *Project for a Revolution in New York*.
A Sentimental Novel.

AUGUSTO ROA BASTOS, *I the Supreme*.

DANIËL ROBBERECHTS, *Arriving in Avignon*.

JEAN ROLIN, *The Explosion of the Radiator Hose*.

OLIVIER ROLIN, *Hotel Crystal*.

ALIX CLEO ROUBAUD, *Alix's Journal*.

JACQUES ROUBAUD, *The Form of a City Changes Faster, Alas, Than the Human Heart*.
The Great Fire of London.
Hortense in Exile.
Hortense Is Abducted.
Mathematics: The Plurality of Worlds of Lewis.
Some Thing Black.

LLORENÇ VILLALONGA, *The Dolls'
Room.*

TOOMAS VINT, *An Unending Landscape.*

ORNELA VORPSI, *The Country Where No
One Ever Dies.*

AUSTRYN WAINHOUSE, *Hedyphagetica.*

CURTIS WHITE, *America's Magic
Mountain.*
The Idea of Home.
Memories of My Father Watching TV.
Requiem.

DIANE WILLIAMS,
Excitability: Selected Stories.
Romancer Erector.

DOUGLAS WOOLF, *Wall to Wall.*
Ya! & John-Juan.

JAY WRIGHT, *Polynomials and Pollen.*
The Presentable Art of Reading Absence.

PHILIP WYLIE, *Generation of Vipers.*

MARGUERITE YOUNG, *Angel in the
Forest.*
Miss MacIntosh, My Darling.

REYOUNG, *Unbabbling.*

VLADO ŽABOT, *The Succubus.*

ZORAN ŽIVKOVIĆ , *Hidden Camera.*

LOUIS ZUKOFSKY, *Collected Fiction.*

VITOMIL ZUPAN, *Minuet for Guitar.*

SCOTT ZWIREN, *God Head.*

AND MORE . . .